THE VAMPIRE KNITTING CLUB

FIRST IN A PARANORMAL COZY MYSTERY SERIES

Nancy Warren

AMBLESIDE PUBLISHING

The Vampire Knitting Club
Copyright © 2018 Nancy Weatherley Warren
All rights reserved

Discover other titles by Nancy Warren at
www.NancyWarren.net

ONE

CARDINAL WOOLSEY'S KNITTING shop has appeared on postcards celebrating the quaint views of Oxford, of which there are many. When a visitor has tired of writing 'wish you were here' on the back of pictures of the various colleges, the dreaming spires, and the dome of the Radcliffe Camera, a cozy little shop painted blue, brimming with baskets of wool and hand-knitted goods, can be so much more inviting.

My grandmother, Agnes Bartlett, owned the best knitting shop in Oxford and I was on my way to visit her after spending a very hot month at a dig site in Egypt with my archeologist parents.

I was looking forward to telling Gran about my latest life crisis. I might be twenty-seven years old and supposedly all grown up, but Gran was always ready to wrap her warm arms around me and tell me everything was going to be all right. I needed comforting after discovering my boyfriend of two years, Todd, had stuck his salami in someone else's sandwich. I referred to him now as my ex-boyfriend 'The Toad.'

I was thinking how much I needed Gran's wisdom, her hugs, and her homemade gingersnaps as I walked down Cornmarket Street toward Ship Street. A busker played his guitar and sang Bob Dylan, not very successfully as suggested by the small number of coins in his open guitar case. I dodged out of the way before a tour group swallowed me whole. As I passed, the tour guide was pointing out the three storey timber-framed building on the corner where it leans drunkenly into the street. "Built in 1386, for a local wine merchant, this was originally called the New Inn." I'd moved past, then, and couldn't hear anymore. I'd learned a lot about Oxford from overhearing snatches of tours. One day, I should really take one.

Just past Ship Street, I turned into Harrington Street where Gran's yarn shop is located. After the bustle and crowds of Cornmarket, it seemed quiet and nearly deserted.

My case bounced and rattled as I crossed the patch of cobblestones in front of Cardinal College. A sign outside the arched entrance informed me that the college was closed to visitors today. It wasn't not the main entrance to the college, but it still featured fierce gargoyles glaring down over the pale gold Headington stone façade, and through the gate I glimpsed the quad with a fountain in its center. I continued, following the college wall to its end, passing a row of parked bicycles, and then to the commercial part of Harrington where the shops were.

They weren't as old as the colleges. They were

Georgian, mostly, standing like a row of elegant ladies, in cream or the palest pastel shades. They contain shops at street level and flats above. Cardinal Woolsey's is in the middle of the commercial section, with a pale green plaster front, and the original sash windows, all painted white. The shop has one big front window and a door with a glass front. All the shop woodwork is painted bright blue. The window frames a display of richly colored wools, an antique spinning wheel, usually draped with a hand knit or crocheted blanket, a selection of books, kits and usually a gorgeous sweater or two.

Suddenly, I started to feel as though cold, wet fingers were walking down the back of my neck.

The September day was mild and I was warm since I'd walked from the train station. When I looked ahead, I saw two ladies on the other side of the street headed toward me. One of them was Gran. She was wearing a black skirt, sensible shoes and one of her hand-knitted cardigans, this one in orange and blue. With her was a glamorous woman in her sixties whom I didn't recognize. I called out and waved. They both wore wide-brimmed hats and, as I started forward, they ducked their chins so their faces were hidden from me. Still, I'd know my grandmother anywhere.

I called again, "Gran!" moving faster so my suitcase began to bounce.

I was sure they saw me, but as I sped toward them, they veered down Rook Lane, a narrow passageway that connects Harrington to George Street. What on earth? I lifted my case and began to run, though my case was so heavy it was more of a grunting stagger.

"Gran!" I yelled again. I ran to the bottom of the alley they'd turned into, but there was no one there. A dry, shriveled leaf tumbled toward across the flagstones me and from a window ledge a small, black cat regarded me, with what looked like pity. Otherwise, Rook Lane was empty. "Agnes Bartlett!" I yelled at the top of my lungs.

I stood, panting. The lane was lined with ancient half-timbered Tudor houses mixed with Victorian cottages. She was visiting in one of those homes, presumably. I wondered if it belonged to her glamorous friend.

I followed them down the flagstone'd alley. There was a black wooden door set into the wall beneath a gothic arch. It was just shutting as I reached it. I contemplated ringing the small brass bell, but didn't want to make a fool of myself so resisted and walked on. There was no sign of Gran.

Well, there was no point hanging around in a deserted lane. I'd go to Cardinal Woolsey's and wait for Gran there. Her assistant, Rosemary, would be working and I could let myself into the upstairs flat and unpack while I waited for my grandmother to return.

I couldn't wait to tell Gran the news about my broken heart, knowing I'd get more sympathy and understanding than I got from Mom, who, even when she looked at me, still seemed to be thinking of times and people long gone. I've always found it difficult to compete with the mysteries of the ancient world, but

Gran listens with her whole attention and says exactly the right thing.

I think the only disappointment for both of us is that she's never been able to teach me to knit. Everything I try, whether it's a sweater, a pair of socks or a simple scarf ends up looking like a scrunched-up hedgehog.

I got to the entrance of the quaint blue-fronted shop and tried the door. It didn't open. I tried again, pushing harder before my other senses kicked in and I realized there were no lights on inside.

A printed sign hung on the windowed front door that said, "Cardinal Woolsey's is closed until further notice." At the bottom was a phone number.

Closed until further notice?

I pressed my face against the window in the door, but everything was dark. Where was Rosemary? Gran never closed the shop outside of her posted closing days. And why was there a fan of mail on the floor? It looked as no one had picked it up in weeks.

When I straightened and looked down the street again, a teenaged girl walked by and stared at me through narrowed eyes. She looked like a goth, with a pale face, dark, heavily made up eyes and long black hair. Her outfit was also all black, including the umbrella shielding her. It was a dry day with no hint of rain. Perhaps she was one of those people who always liked to be prepared. No doubt she had snow boots in the tapestry bag she carried, and sunscreen in case the sun should decide to shine.

I turned back to the shop and wondered what to do. There wasn't much communication at the dig site and I hadn't thought to check ahead and make sure Gran had remembered I was coming. She always remembered. I stood there gnawing my lip. I stepped back, almost into the road and looked up but I couldn't see lights on in the flat, either.

The proper entrance to the flat is off the lane behind the shop. So, dragging my case behind me once more, I continued on, past Pennyfarthing Antiques. I noted the still life oil painting of the bowl of fruit and the dead fish was still displayed, as it had been when I was last here six months ago, along with a bowfront chest supporting a silver tea set. Past that was the pub on the corner, The Bishop's Mitre. The date 1588 was carved into the wooden lintel of the pub, which served ale to King Charles II when he was in hiding during the English Civil War. It calls itself a gastropub now.

I dragged my bag back toward the pub once more, to Hall Street. Across from me was St. John's church with its ancient graveyard. I rounded the corner, walked past the side of the pub and turned down the lane that ran behind the row of shops.

The lane was barely wide enough for one car and featured plenty of No Parking signs. When I got to Gran's place, her tiny, ancient car was sitting in the equally tiny parking spot she managed to wedge the vehicle into. I opened the wooden gate and walked up the path through the small back garden. Gran grew wildflowers and herbs, mostly, but the beds looked overgrown and in need of water. As I walked down the narrow, winding path to her door, my leg brushed against lavender that had bushed out into the path. I stopped for a moment, enjoying the scents of rosemary and lavender, thyme and roses, and the sounds of fat, happy bees who didn't seem to mind that the garden was a mess.

When I got to the door, I pressed the intercom, just in case someone was there. No one answered. I tried a second time, holding my finger on the button that would ring upstairs, but there was still nothing.

I pulled out my phone, but I don't know why I bothered. I didn't have a UK plan yet. I left my suitcase tucked against the door, and walked back around to Harrington Street and past the yarn shop. Next door was Elderflower Tea Shop.

The two Miss Watts who owned the tea shop had been pouring tea and baking scones and other English delicacies for decades, possibly centuries. They knew everyone and everything about the neighborhood. Also, they were both close friends of my grandmother. If she was out visiting, I could wait for her here.

As I walked into the warm and familiar tea shop, the elder Miss Watt, Mary, glanced up at me. Her face had that 'yes, can I help you?' expression, which quickly changed to sorrow when she recognized me. "Oh, Lucy, is that you?"

"Yes. How are you, Miss Watt?"

"I'm fine, dear." She didn't look fine, though. She

looked worried verging on panicked. She glanced around as though she could summon help, but, other than herself, there was no one in the shop but me and a family of French tourists.

"Gran's not home. I thought I'd wait for her here." She put her hands over her mouth and then stepped around from behind the counter and ushered me to a table as far from her only other customers as she could get. "Then, you haven't heard. Sit down, dear. Let me get you some tea."

The mild unease I'd felt deepened. "Heard what? What's going on?"

She shook her head slowly. When her eyes filled with tears I felt my stomach clench in dread. The hard wood of the seat bumped against my butt as I sat without realizing I was going to. As rump bumped wood, she said, "I'm so sorry, Lucy. Your grandmother passed away."

"No." I whispered the word. "That's impossible. I just saw her, on the street."

Sadness was coming off her in waves. She shook her head. "You must have seen someone who looked like her."

I'd been so certain it was Gran. Could I have been mistaken? I recalled the moment when I'd seen her. She hadn't acknowledged me, even though I'd shouted her name and waved. The woman had been wearing a hat, which Gran never did, but she'd looked so much like Gran. "Are you sure?"

She nodded.

Life without Gran was unthinkable. Of course, I'd known she was old and would die sometime, but she was a robust woman in her early eighties, showing no signs of slowing down, often boasting that she'd never known a day's illness.

"It was very peaceful," Mary Watt said. "She died in her sleep. And she wasn't a young woman."

"But she wasn't old. Not really. And she was always so healthy." Maybe if I hadn't seen that woman who was a dead ringer for Gran I wouldn't be having so much trouble accepting she was gone.

"It's how we all want to go, isn't it? Healthy to the last and then one day to go to bed and not wake up." Mary Watt was very close in age to my gran. She wasn't only making polite conversation. She really wanted to go that way.

I sat there, staring at the oak tabletop. I didn't hear Miss Watt move and I was in the same position when she reappeared with a Brown Betty pot of tea, two cups, and one of their famous scones served with jam and clotted cream.

She poured me a cup and then sat down and poured herself the second cup. "Drink your tea, dear. And try the scone. You're probably hungry."

I couldn't eat. Because it gave me something to do, I picked up the cup and drank some tea. The brew was strong and hot, and I sipped for a few minutes as I absorbed the terrible news.

Miss Watt kept her wide-eyed gaze on me. Her gray hair was coiled in a tidy bun at the back of her neck, as always. Her face was kind and sad. Her faded blue eyes regarded me with sympathy.

"I don't know what to do," I said at last. "There was a phone number on the notice stuck to Gran's store but my phone doesn't work here."

She nodded sympathetically. Then jumped to her feet as though pleased to be able to offer concrete help. "You can use our phone. That number will get you to her lawyer, I think."

"Will it?" I was having trouble concentrating. It felt like she was talking to me from a long way away.

"I imagine so. Anyway, you must stay with me and Florence while you sort things out. We have a nice cozy guest room upstairs."

As much as I appreciated the kindness of the two sisters, I knew that I needed to be in Gran's home while I digested the news. "Thank you. That's really nice of you. But, if I could use your phone, I'll call the lawyer and see if I can get the keys today."

"Well, of course you can call from here. But, we've got the keys to your grandmother's shop and the flat upstairs. We always kept each other's keys you know."

She patted my hand, then went behind the cash desk and returned with a set of keys on a round brass ring. It wasn't until I was leaving that I turned to her and asked the question I should've asked much earlier. "When did Gran die?"

"About three weeks ago. No one could get hold of you or your mother. I'm so sorry."

When I let myself into Gran's knitting shop the first

thing I noticed was that familiar scent. Cardinal Woolsey's smelled like wool and old stone. And, if gossip had a scent, I could smell all the secrets that had been shared over knitting patterns and classes. Everyone had loved my grandmother. Friends and customers brought their problems to her and their stories. She gave good advice, but most of all, she was an excellent listener. Simply talking to her made you feel better.

I gazed at the baskets of wool stacked on shelves, and at the knitting porn — those gorgeous pattern books and magazines featuring beautiful women complicated sweaters and shawls I'm sure no human could knit. Certainly not me. As I looked around, I felt such a sense of nostalgia and sadness that I had to hang onto the counter to steady myself. The silence felt as heavy as my grief.

I picked up the small stack of mail that had collected, placed it on the wooden counter, then I let myself through the door that connected to the flat upstairs, flipping on lights as I went. The upstairs flat was on two floors. On the main was an old-fashioned kitchen, a sitting room, dining room and a study cum TV room. Above that were two bedrooms and bathroom.

It smelled musty, like an old house that's been shut up during the summer. I opened windows, then went back down the back stairs, retrieved my suitcase, and hauled it up the steps to the second bedroom, which I always thought of as mine. Gran had let me decorate the room when I was a teenager and I still liked the lilac walls and the purple-flowered bedding. On the wall was a poster of Miley Cyrus, in her pre-twerking days, and another of The Spice Girls. My eyes filled with tears when I saw that the bed was all made up ready for me. There were fresh towels on the bed. Gran had been looking forward to my arrival.

I walked back downstairs to the kitchen. I wasn't hungry, but I needed something to occupy me. I opened the fridge and the cupboards randomly. Someone had tossed the perishable food items, but there were her favorite biscuits and a half jar of the marmalade she always used.

I had to really gather my courage to walk into her bedroom. Strangely, though she had died there, I had the least sense of her in that room. The bedding had been stripped down to the mattress, and the room seemed oddly impersonal.

Why couldn't she have waited? If she was going to die, I should have been here.

I busied myself with unpacking and then walked to the convenience store on the corner, The Full Stop. There I stocked up on milk, eggs, a loaf of bread and some fruit. When I got home I made myself some toast and sat thinking, remembering mostly, until the church bells chimed ten o'clock and I decided to go to bed.

I don't know if it was jet lag or grief but I found myself wide awake at two in the morning, the kind of wide awake where you know there's no point banging your head against the pillow because you won't be falling asleep again.

I got out of bed and realized I needed to do something. I was full of restless energy. I wanted to cry and scream and break things, instead I dressed in jeans and an old sweater, shoved my feet into sneakers and went downstairs to the shop. I flipped on lights and then walked around almost mindlessly tidying and straightening.

One of the charms of Cardinal Woolsey's was that it never changed. I knew exactly where everything should be because it had always been there.

However, as I tidied up, I realized that the basket of Fair Isle knitting wool had somehow shifted to the area where mohair should be. I swapped the baskets back to the correct places.

Gran was always meticulous about keeping her shop clean as well as tidy so I grabbed a duster and went to work. When I finished the dusting I pulled out the vacuum cleaner and got to work on the old wooden plank floor. I was pushing the wand into a corner when I caught the gleam of gold. I dropped to my knees and reached under the bottom shelf and discovered Gran's eyeglasses. She'd always kept them on a gold chain around her neck, but the chain was broken.

I held them in my hands feeling a shudder of sadness go through me and something else. The chain ran through my fingers again and again. As though in a dream, I had the feeling of fear and something terrible chasing me, but no sense of what the thing was. My heart was pounding when my vision cleared.

I searched the area and noticed a line of black

splatters on the old hardwood floor. Could be paint, could be nail polish but, as the daughter of two archaeologists, I knew the importance of investigating small details. I dampened a tissue and rubbed carefully at the largest spot. A rusty brown came up on the tissue. I'm not much of an expert in forensics but I was fairly certain it was blood.

Here's the thing. My grandmother was close to blind without her glasses on, especially at night. So I had to ask myself, if she had died peacefully in her bed, as Miss Watt had told me, then why were her broken glasses downstairs in the shop? Along with recently spilled blood?

Two

I WAS CROUCHED down, staring at the lenses of my grandmother's glasses, my mind working furiously, when I felt a cold draft. The back of my neck prickled and I shivered. Gran would have said someone had just walked over my grave.

It wasn't a noise that made me glance up, not even a movement. It felt more like a presence. The kind that would make me sometimes flip on a light when I woke in the night from one of my dreams, heart pounding as it was beginning to pound now.

Of course when I switched my light on at home, it was always to the reassuring sight of my own bedroom with no monsters, serial killers, or otherwise scary dudes in my space.

This time I wasn't so lucky.

There was a man standing inside the door. I must have made a sound, though I'd have sworn I was too frightened even to breathe. He turned quickly, and I felt he was as startled to see me as I was to see him. But seen me he undoubtedly had, so I rose to my feet, trying to beat back the panic.

"Who are you?" I asked. I wanted to sound tough and controlled but even I could hear my voice waver.

"Where's Agnes?" he retorted.

"Agnes?" I was surprised she'd know a man like this.

"Yes." He sounded impatient and took a step forward. "Agnes Bartlett."

I wasn't about to tell him that my grandmother was dead, not when he'd appeared out of nowhere in the middle of the night, so I asked again, "Who are you?"

He stepped forward. He was tall, lean, and elegant. About thirty-five or so. He wore black slacks and a dark gray sweater, but the way he wore it, the outfit could have been a tuxedo. His hair was black, his eyes dark, and his face pale. He fascinated and repelled me at once.

"My name is Rafe Crosyer."

I followed up with a second, more important question, "How did you get in?"

He hesitated. "I saw the light. I was passing and thought Agnes might need something."

If he knew my grandmother, how did he not know she'd passed away? And why was he strolling past in the middle of the night? "Do you live in the neighborhood?"

He glanced behind me as though I might have my grandmother hidden somewhere. "Yes. But I've been out of town. Is she here?"

I licked dry lips. "Maybe you should come back tomorrow."

His brow creased. "You're holding her glasses, and

the chain appears to be broken."

The chain made a noise as my hands shook as much from grief as from fear. I wondered if I was in the middle of some elaborate dream. Maybe Gran wasn't dead, and I wasn't having a bizarre conversation with a strange man in the middle of the night holding my grandmother's broken glasses. "Do you often visit her in the middle of the night?"

A flicker of something crossed his face. Irritation? Amusement? "I suffer from insomnia. Your grandmother is also a sufferer." He smiled slightly at my obvious shock that he'd referred to her as my grandmother. "Lucy, I presume. Your grandmother often speaks of you. I've seen your photograph."

Maybe she'd spoken of me to him but I was positive my grandmother had never mentioned tall-dark-and-snooty. I'd have remembered. Still, if he knew her so well, I was tempted to tell him what had happened. But I'd spent too much time in chaotic cities, warned by my parents never to talk to strangers, to unburden myself. Not at three in the morning when I was all alone.

He'd been watching me fiddle with the broken chain. "Your grandmother can't see two feet in front of her without those glasses." He took a step back and deliberately relaxed his pose. "I only want to know that she's all right."

"Please," I said, "Come back tomorrow."

He hesitated. "I'll be in meetings all day. I'll come tomorrow evening. After sunset."

"Whatever."

He smiled at that. "Until tomorrow evening then."

He reached into his pocket and I flinched thinking of all the things a scary guy could pull out of his pocket, but his hand emerged holding nothing more lethal than a business card. "If you need anything, call me at this number. Day or night."

I reached for the card as he passed it forward, and our hands brushed. "Your hands are so cold," I said. It's a bit of a problem I have when I'm nervous. I blab whatever I'm thinking.

He drew back and flexed his fingers. "Poor circulation." He walked back to the door. "Good night."

"Wait, how did you get in?" He still hadn't explained how he'd appeared inside the shop.

He paused. "The door was unlocked."

I'm not sure of a lot of things in life, like what a guy means when he says, "I'll call you," or whether my hair looks better long or short, but I was damned sure I'd locked that door before I went up to bed.

Damned sure.

* * *

After the scary guy left, I made triple sure that outder door was locked, and the one that led to the flat, and then I went back upstairs. I carried Gran's broken glasses with me, wishing they could talk. Something wasn't right. Why were her glasses broken and in the shop if she'd died peacefully in bed? And since when was she pally with was a strange man who walked into the shop in the wee hours without so much as knocking?

Rafe Crosyer was seriously hot. I'd have suspected

her late night caller had more than knitting in mind, but as far as I knew, she'd never had another man after my grandfather died. Plus, the age difference must be about fifty years, and he did not seem the boy toy type.

I went back to bed but I was so unnerved, I got up and turned on the bathroom light, leaving my bedroom door open so I wouldn't be shut up in the dark. My room no longer felt like a safe, comfortable refuge. Every noise, whether inside or out, had me opening my eyes wide to search out any possible danger until exhaustion finally claimed me and I slept.

When I woke, the sun was shining and I looked out my window to the skyline that could be nowhere but Oxford. They may call the gathering of church steeples 'dreaming spires' but they'd interrupted my dreams throughout the night, chiming the hour. It always took me a couple of nights to get used to bells ringing every hour on the hour all night long.

I glanced at my phone and found it was after eleven. I felt thick and stupid and desperate for that first cup of coffee, but at least I'd slept.

I stumbled to the kitchen, put on coffee, and while it brewed, so did my thoughts. Gran's glasses, blood on the floor, the strange visitor last night. Put those things together, and I came to any number of disturbing possibilities, none of which made any sense.

What I needed, and badly, was information.

The first thing I had to do was to phone the number on the sign on the door. I'd been too stunned to do it yesterday. Gran had never owned a mobile phone that I knew of. She had actual wall phones. One in the store and one in her apartment above. I'd snapped a photo of the sign on the door and, as soon as I'd drunk my first cup of strong coffee, I sucked in a breath and called the number.

"*Mills, Tate and Elliot*, how may I direct your call?" a pleasant female voice enquired.

"I found this number on a sign taped to Cardinal Woolsey's, the knitting shop on Harrington Street. The owner was my grandmother."

"Please hold," she said, and the line clicked.

In a few seconds, an older male voice said, "George Tate speaking."

Once more, I explained about the note and the number.

"And what is your name?" he asked.

"Lucy Agnes Swift." Yes, Agnes for my grandmother.

"Miss Swift, I am very sorry to inform you that your grandmother passed away several weeks ago. I'd very much like to speak to you. When would it be convenient to come to our offices?"

Fortunately, my grandmother had employed an Oxford firm of lawyers within walking distance of the shop, so we agreed that I would stop by at two that afternoon.

"And please bring official identification with you," he said before ringing off.

I took a shower in the old-fashioned bathroom, climbing into the big tub and banging my shin as I did every single time I returned to Gran's place. It always took me a few bruises to get the bath climbing routine down.

I showered, left my long blonde hair to dry on its own, brushed my teeth, put on mascara and lipstick, and dressed in my best jeans and a long-sleeved cotton T-shirt. When I'd flown out of Cairo the temperature had been sweltering. Here it was approaching sweater weather.

Somehow, I needed to get hold of my mother and let her know that Gran was gone. But, I decided to see the lawyer first and find out as much as I could.

According to Miss Watt and the lawyer, my grandmother had died weeks ago. I must have missed her funeral. Somehow, missing the burial made everything more painful. I hadn't had a chance to say goodbye. I would have to find out where she was buried and at least take some flowers. I needed closure.

I glanced at the glasses on their broken chain, which I seemed to keep carrying around with me as though Gran might suddenly appear and ask for them. I needed more than a gravesite to visit. I needed answers.

I'd placed the business card the strange man had given me last night on the kitchen counter and I picked it up now. The card stock was plain but expensive. Rafe William Crosyer. And a phone number, mobile phone, email address and a website.

According to his card, he was an antiquarian book and restoration expert. I would definitely be checking out his website before I saw him again. I'm good like that, checking up on strange men who walk in on me in the middle of the night.

The offices of Mills, Tate and Elliot occupied Victorian brick storefront on New Inn Hall Street, only five minutes' walk away. I opened the old oak door and expected to find a clerk writing with a quill pen, but to my relief the inside of the law office was quite modern. The receptionist might sit behind a counter older than some countries, but she punched my details into a slick computer and then asked me to take a seat. I'd barely picked up a copy of *The Economist* when a thin, elegant man in his sixties wearing a navy suit stepped toward me. "Miss Swift?"

"Yes." I rose and shook his hand, and he led me to an office that looked like a professor's lair. It was lined with books, and the heavy, ornate desk was covered in paper. There was no computer in this office. Only a phone. I could see why my grandmother had hired him.

I sat on one side of the desk and Mr. Tate sat on the other. He stared at me so long I had to force myself not to fidget. "Did you bring your identification?"

"Yes." I tugged both my passports from my bag. I'm a dual citizen, having been born in Oxford to my British mother and American father, and having lived most of my life in the States. My father was an American lecturer in Oxford when he met my mother who was a student there. They moved to Massachusetts when I was still a baby, but worked on dig sites all over the world. I'd spent most of my summers with my grandmother in Oxford, and they'd been some of my happiest times.

"Excellent. I'll have these copied." He poked his head out the door and the woman at the front fetched them.

Then he sat back, shook his head, and sighed. "Well, my dear, I'm sorry for your loss. Your grandmother was a wonderful woman."

"She was. Did you know her well?"

"We met now and again socially. We were both friends of the Bodleian Library. My firm did all her legal work, what there was of it."

"Of course."

He pulled a file forward and opened it. "Are you at all familiar with your grandmother's will?"

"No. Not at all."

"She never discussed it with you?"

I shook my head. "Why would she discuss her will with me? My mother must be her heir. She only had the one child."

"Agnes did not leave her estate to her daughter. She left everything to you. She also left you a letter."

He withdrew a sheaf of papers from the file, and a sealed envelope that he pushed across the desktop toward me. I recognized the loopy handwriting and felt a great sweep of sadness. I picked up the envelope, knowing I wouldn't read it in the lawyer's presence. I'd wait until I was alone.

He resettled his gold-rimmed glasses over his nose and scanned pages as though he were reminding himself of the contents. Then he began. "Your grandmother's

23

estate consists of the shop and the living quarters above it. In that part of town, the property is worth quite a pretty sum. Other than that she had some savings and, of course, the income from Cardinal Woolsey's. All this is to go to you."

"But what about my mother?" I was already struggling to accept my grandmother's death, to think of inheriting her property—well, I didn't have room in my brain for more shocks.

"I imagine your grandmother's reasoning will be explained in that letter."

I was certain my mother would not grudge me the shop. She and my father were much too busy with their research to be bothered with it, but I'd never considered that I might one day be asked to run a knitting shop. I was twenty-seven years old and not at all sure what I wanted to do with my life.

I was at a crossroads.

I'd worked for a couple of years in administration for a pharmaceutical firm, sitting in a cubicle for eight hours a day. The atmosphere was so dull, the cactus I brought into work died. I was certain it died of boredom. My entire department was made redundant, which was good as it meant I didn't have to sit in that cubicle anymore, and bad as I had no income. I was still reeling from that shock when, a few days later, on a Friday evening, Todd pocket-dialed me. I answered, but instead of hearing him speak to me, I heard him panting and muttering something over and over again that sounded like, "Oh, yeah, baby."

Todd had told me he was playing poker with the boys. It didn't sound like poker was the game going on, so I got into my car and drove the short distance to his basement suite where I discovered Todd and a girl he worked with going at it on the kitchen table. I've often thought since that if Todd had taken off his jeans all the way, we might still be going out.

This trip had been partly a way to get over the humiliation of Todd's betrayal, as well as an opportunity to figure out what I really wanted to do with my life. I had no idea what a tidy sum might mean, but I was hopeful that if I sold the shop, I might have enough to live on for a while until I found my path.

Mr. Tate was speaking, and I was listening, even as these thoughts were going through my head. At last, he said, "And now we reach the conditions of your inheritance."

"Conditions?"

"Yes. They aren't very onerous, but your grandmother requested two things. One, that you run the shop yourself, for at least a year, and two, that you must keep it exactly as it is."

"Or what?" I had to ask.

He took off his glasses and polished them. "Legally, you can do whatever you want with the property. These are requests from your grandmother."

I'd come looking for a purpose in life, but I couldn't see myself running a knitting shop. Mr. Tate looked at me, waiting for me to speak. I could only think of one thing that was relevant.

"But I don't know how to knit."

THREE

I SHOOK MR. TATE'S hand and left his office feeling
stunned. My brain was crowded with questions as his
receptionist returned my passports and wished me a
pleasant day.

I pushed open the large double doors that had *Mills
Tate & Elliot, Solicitors* stenciled in gold letters. When I
got back onto the street, a draft of cool air tousled my
hair, refreshing my mind and helping to calm my
thoughts. Why would Gran have specified that Cardinal
Woolsey's must remain a knitting shop? I knew the
shop was important to her; Gran had inherited it from
her mother, so it had been in the family for over a
generation, but, at the end of the day, it was a knitting
shop. She knew I couldn't knit. Why would she care
what I did with it?

Sure, I'd helped her out in the shop while my
parents were scraping ancient dust off of priceless
antiquities in the middle of the desert, and I did know
my way around quite well. I was probably the only
person other than Gran's assistant, Rosemary, who

knew how to run the place, but I was hardly a shopkeeper. And I didn't even live in Oxford!

Plus there was my complete ineptitude around knitting. Gran tried to teach me once, but somehow my simple knit-two-purl-two scarf kept curling itself up into intricate knots and bunching into unusual shapes every time I took my eyes off it.

"Well now, I've never seen a scarf turn out quite like that." Gran had laughed, unperturbed by the fact that my winter scarf had transformed into a sea urchin.

I tossed it in the corner and Gran's cat ate holes in it. He died shortly afterward and, even though he was an old cat, I always felt like my knitting might have done him in.

Without Gran here to guide my hand, I doubted I'd knit another stitch.

I headed down George Street with her precious letter clutched in my hand. I felt so lost. Seeing people in groups, whether of students, bus-sized clusters of tourists, or couples arm in arm, I also felt lonely. I'd planned to talk to Gran about my future and what I should do with it.

There'd been a small payout when I was made redundant. My parents had urged me to go back to school. I'd thought I might travel a bit. Maybe walking in Spain, or lying on beach in Thailand. I'd never considered running Cardinal Woolsey's. Or living in Oxford permanently.

I turned right onto Worcester Street and past Worcester College. Late summer roses rambled up the biscuit colored walls and the lawn looked recently mowed and as untried as the Freshers who'd be starting college soon.

Worchester turned into Walton Street and headed into Jericho, one of my favorite parts of Oxford. It was less touristy and filled with cafes and little restaurants. I passed Oxford University Press, as timeless and elegant as a Penguin classic. Traffic was backed up and only the cyclists went faster than me.

A cyclist wheeled in front of me to the business college that looked like a spaceship that landed in the middle of this ancient city, and behind it I glimpsed the dome of the neoclassical Oxford Observatory, which I'd seen as a backdrop for countless British TV dramas.

I contemplated popping into The Jericho Café and sitting over coffee while I read my letter, but my feet kept going and I knew I needed to be in nature. I headed to Port Meadow, a large green space which meanders beside the River Thames. On a Tuesday afternoon there was no one but me and a few joggers and dog walkers. I followed the river for a while and then I sat down on a wooden bench, took a deep breath, and opened Gran's letter.

My Dearest Lucy,

If you are reading this letter then I am gone. I've lived a good life and I am quite at peace, and grateful to have shared with you the time that we had.

I am so proud of you and everything that I know you will accomplish in your life. You are still young, but know that you have a great power within you. You are stronger than you know, and you will soon discover that you are capable of a great many things, which you may now believe are impossible. All will be revealed in time, but for now just know that you must stay strong. There will be challenges ahead. I am sorry I cannot be there to prepare you. In times of darkness, seek the light within. You will know what to do.

Seek the light within? What challenges?

I'm leaving all my worldly possessions to you, Lucy. I've left a letter for your mother, but she always knew I intended you to have the shop. Please keep Cardinal Woolsey's exactly as it currently stands. I ask that you not sell or change it, and you will shortly find out why.

Why couldn't she have *told* me why? And Mom had known all along that this was going to happen? Why didn't one of them tell me? This letter didn't clear up anything at all.

I'm sure you still have questions—some of the answers can be found in our family diary. The big, leather-bound book I once showed you. Keep an open mind as you read it. You'll find out more about your family if you can decipher the clues.

I love you dearly, Lucy, and trust that you will do your best to respect my wishes. Find the book and do not change the shop. Stay strong and keep an open mind. I have a feeling you'll be making some rather special new friends here in Oxford before long.

Your loving grandmother,

Agnes Bartlett

A spaniel ran up to me, nosing the paper I held on my lap, no doubt hoping it was a dog treat. That brought me back to my senses and I patted the black head. The dog ran off as soon as it understood that treats would not be forthcoming. I read the letter again. It was written on sheets of elegant stationary, with a decorative motif of faded wildflowers and blue curlicues adorning one corner.

Had I somehow misread her words? No, the graceful loops of Gran's cursive hand were as precise as ever. When I reread the letter the meaning was the same. What meaning I could glean. Gran wanted me to run her knitting shop and spend my spare time reading an ancient family diary I barely remembered. And I thought my life in the corporate cubicle had been dull.

I folded up Gran's letter and placed it back in its envelope with a sigh. I sat for a moment longer staring out into the river, watching a trio of white swans float past. I got up to leave, heading back to the city just as confused as ever.

When I returned to Cardinal Woolsey's, I'd decided the first thing I'd better do was an inventory. I wasn't sure I'd stay a year, or even a month, but I ought to figure out what was there. I still couldn't figure out why everything had been so disordered. I'd have to talk to Rosemary Johnson, Gran's assistant. She must know what was going on.

I made a start right away on the inventory. It helped keep me occupied while I let the contents of Gran's will and her letter sink in. It didn't take me long to notice that the knitting needles weren't hung according to size and that tubular needles were hanging under a sign advertising miscellaneous buttons. A jumble of needlework threads had been thrust into a bowl on the cash desk like a dish of candy. It would take me ages to sort and put them back into the correct drawers.

I found cranberry wool mixed with maroon, Alpaca Classic pushed into the same cubby as Alpaca Merino. To the casual observer, the shop probably looked fine,, but to someone doing inventory, it was chaos. To a knitter, the muddled wools would be maddening.

I had to wonder if Gran's mind had been going in her final days.

But if that was so, how come the upstairs apartment was so orderly? Gran had clearly cleaned it up and prepared it for my arrival. If she had taken the time to spruce up the guestroom, wouldn't she have made sure to also have the shop in order?

I'd helped her computerize the inventory, but she liked to keep printouts, never completely trusting computers. Under the cash register, the desk held one cupboard and three small shelves. The bottom two shelves held nothing but a bit of dust, and the top one contained a few papers as well as a handful of peppermints that looked like they had seen better days. Inside the cupboard, I found the leather-bound special order book that contained order forms—and yes, there was the most recent inventory.

The shrill toll of the shop's front bell rang, startling me in the quiet. I'd forgotten to lock the door, but still, the closed sign hung on the door. Anybody who couldn't read a sign that said CLOSED probably didn't see well enough to knit.

"Hellooo!" a woman's voice called, the end of the word unnaturally extended in a lilting sing-song jingle that trailed off into an unspoken question mark. "Is anyone here?"

I stood up awkwardly from behind the counter. "Hi. Can I help you?"

The woman standing before me was of indeterminate age. There was a crinkling at the corners of her eyes and a slight sag to her jawline, but her skin was tight, her hair styled into a bob and sprayed down so hard it looked as though you could take a mallet to her hair and not crack it. She held herself in a confident pose with a straight back and an expectant smile.

She wore a black dress and a smart black and gray jacket. I was impressed that she could wear heels that high without keeling over. Tucked under her arm was a slim black leather attaché case. "I didn't mean to startle you," she said effusively. "Is Agnes here? It's Sidney Lafontaine to see her."

She came towards me and leaned forward, peering at me intently from sparkling blue eyes, getting a little too close for my comfort.

A pang of sadness swept over me at her words. "I guess you haven't heard. Agnes passed away."

The woman's black-lined eyes popped open in surprise at my words, and she brought her hand to her mouth in an expression of shock. "Passed? You mean—"

"She's dead." I said the words she didn't seem able to mouth. I found that euphemisms like *passed away* and *crossed the rainbow bridge* hurt just as much as plain old 'dead.'

"Good heavens, it can't be. I only saw her a few weeks ago. Are you quite sure?"

Who lies about their beloved grandmother being dead? "Yes. I'm sure."

"Oh dear, this is dreadful news." She seemed to be thinking rapidly. "Did she talk to you about her plans for the future?"

I wondered if this woman was some kind of an ambulance chaser. Was there such a thing as a hearse chaser? All I knew was that I instinctively recoiled from this woman. "May I ask how you knew my grandmother?" The woman didn't look like a knitter. She hadn't even glanced at the contents of the shop.

"It's a little delicate. Are you a relative?"

I hesitated, but I couldn't see that me being Agnes's granddaughter should be a big secret, so I told her about our relationship. She nodded. Then asked if my parents were in town.

When I told her they weren't, she tapped red painted fingernails against her case. I was finding this conversation tedious and uncomfortable. "Is there something I can help you with?"

"Yes. Do you know who is handling your grandmother's affairs? My business is with Agnes Bartlett's beneficiaries."

I could send her to George Tate who would

probably be very discreet, but since I'm fairly certain wills are public documents she'd end up back here, eventually. On the other hand, my mother didn't even know about the will yet. I wasn't going to tell this pushy woman that I was the beneficiary before Mom even knew. "Perhaps I could get a message to my mother? She was Agnes's only child."

"Only the one child." I felt she was once more debating with herself. Finally, she said, "I'm an estate agent. I have a client who is interested in buying Cardinal Woolsey's. Your grandmother was very keen to sell, getting on in age, and with no one living close by who was interested in running it."

"Is that so?" *Liar, liar, pants on fire.*

My fingertips started to tingle. I glanced down and saw sparks shooting out of the index finger on my right hand and the ring finger on my left. The static electricity in here must be insane. It had never happened to me before, but maybe the dry air and the wool were having some kind of strange reaction. I rubbed my fingers on my jeans.

She nodded. "I know it's a terrible time for all of Agnes's loved ones, but I'm sure you don't want to be burdened with a knitting shop all the way over here in Oxford. You and your parents should talk it over." She leaned in confidentially, getting into my personal space. "Buyers who are excited tend to pay top dollar."

"What would top dollar be?" I was curious about the value of this property. She glanced around as though she was about to reveal state secrets, and then lowered her voice though the shop was empty but for us. She mentioned an amount that was eye-popping to a girl who'd struggled to pay the rent, groceries and all the bills on her last salary. She looked at me to gauge my reaction and must have liked what she saw because she smiled, smugly. "Talk to your mother and ask her to give me a ring."

I found myself being handed yet another business card, which I took carefully, hoping my fingers wouldn't spark again and start a fire, even though I liked the idea of using her business card as kindling. And then, with a cheerful goodbye, she was off.

Why would Gran give this woman any encouragement if she was determined that I should run the shop after she was gone? Sidney Lafontaine had to be lying. I tapped the edge of the card against the wooden sales counter, frowning. Once more the possibility flitted through my mind that Gran hadn't been entirely herself in the months since I'd seen her.

I locked the door after she left. I had so many things buzzing around in my head I couldn't seem to focus on any one. I closed my eyes and took a deep breath to center myself. And came to a conclusion. I needed to make a list.

There was a pad of paper and a pen upstairs in the desk. I'd made a good start on the inventory and I decided I could take a break. I went upstairs, found paper and pen and began to write, in no particular order, the things that were on my mind. When I was done, I felt a little clearer. I read over my list. It wasn't very long, but every single thing on it was a really hard thing to do.

One: Phone Mom and tell her Gran's dead. *Really not looking forward to that one.*

Two: Explain will to Mom. *Ditto.*

Three: Phone Rosemary. When is she coming back to work? *Don't like Rosemary. Wish I didn't have to.*

Four: Rafe Crosyer. Google search. *I felt a shiver just seeing his name.*

Why had I agreed to meet him this evening? If I'd been more with it I would've told him not to come. Maybe I could find someone to hang out with me, so I wasn't all by myself when he arrived. But even as I had the thought I dismissed it. I was a perfectly capable woman. A tall, dangerously sexy insomniac with poor circulation wasn't going to scare me. At least, not much.

Five: Do I want to run a knitting shop? Research options. Hire manager? *Preferably not Rosemary.*

Six: Find out where Gran is buried. Visit. Flowers. Of every task on the list, this one would be the most difficult. A gravesite visit would confirm that she was gone.

Seven: What happened to her glasses? *Who would know?* Wondering about this led to:

Eight: Visit her doctor and find out what she died of.

I decided to tackle the items on my list one at a time in the order I had written them. Getting hold of my parents was not a simple matter of picking up the phone and dialing. There was a satellite phone at the dig site, mainly for emergencies. I called and left a message with one of the Italian students helping at the site. After he said he would pass the message along, and rang off with a cheerful, *Ciao,* I calculated the chances that he'd remember to give her the message at about fifty-fifty.

I decided a backup to the sat phone would be a good idea. Telling a person by email that her mother was dead seemed cruel, so I crafted a careful message saying I'd arrived safely but had some news and asked her to call me. We weren't the kind of family that called from very long distances for chitchat so she'd know something serious was up.

Once I'd sent the email, I felt better. I'd started to take charge of this crazy mess I was in.

I crossed item one off the list, feeling a small sense of accomplishment. That also pretty much took care of the second item. I'd tell my mother about the will when she called. I'd also tell her about the strange woman who seemed to think Gran wanted to sell the shop, even though Gran's last wishes had been to keep it.

The next item was Rosemary. She'd been Gran's shop assistant for several years now and she'd know all the things I didn't, like whether there were any orders coming in or classes scheduled. A lot of Cardinal Woolsey's business came from giving knitting classes and then providing the supplies for all those budding knitters. Gran had taught a lot of the classes herself. Since I didn't think anyone wanted to learn how to knit a scarf that resembled a sea urchin, I figured I would need to find some new teachers.

If I stayed.

Rosemary's phone number was written in the binder where Gran writes the special orders. I can't say I've ever warmed to Rosemary. She's got a whiny voice and always acts like her life is unfair. Even the way she said, "Hello?" you could tell she expected the caller to deliver bad news.

"Rosemary, this is Lucy Swift, Agnes Bartlett's granddaughter."

"What do you want?" She snarled the question. I've always suspected she never warmed to me, either, but she'd always pretended to be delighted to see me, so the surly attitude was kind of strange.

"I was wondering if you'd be able to come into work on Friday?" I asked. It was Tuesday today, that would give me a few days to get organized.

There was a pause. "You mean at the knitting shop?"

No, at MI-5. "Yes, the knitting shop. Cardinal Woolsey's."

"And why would I do that?" Again with the attitude.

"I really need your help. I know it will be hard without Gran, but she wanted the shop to carry on."

"Where's Agnes?"

Had Rosemary been drinking? "She's dead. She's been gone three weeks. Didn't you know?"

The woman gave a snort of laughter that sounded

like hysteria rather than humor. "Dead. Three weeks." There was another sound like a hastily snuffed giggle. Then, "Yes, of course I knew." There was silence on the line and when she spoke again she seemed to have controlled herself and her words were more appropriate. "I'm so sorry for your loss. This must be a terrible time for you. I haven't been well since your grandmother passed. The doctor says it's grief. I'm so sensitive, you see, things always affect me harder than other people."

"Of course." I rolled my eyes. *Thanks for making Gran's death all about you.*

"I can come in whenever you need me. Would you like me to come in tomorrow at my usual time?"

I had a sudden sense that I should tell her no, but it was an impression, gone so swiftly that I ignored it. I needed Rosemary. I'd have to put my personal feelings aside and start thinking about what was best for Cardinal Woolsey's and the customers who relied on us for their knitting, crochet, and needlework needs. "Friday's fine. I've some things to organize before we open."

"For Agnes's sake, I'll make the effort. I'll be there at nine."

"Thank you."

After I hung up, I stood staring at the phone. That was weird. But then everything since I'd arrived back in Oxford had seemed weird.

Including the next thing on my list: Do a Google search on Rafe Crosyer.

FOUR

I TOOK MY laptop next door to Elderflower Tea Shop. The Watt sisters might look like they belonged in a Brontë novel, but they had something the Brontës never had: high speed Wi-Fi.

Next to Cardinal Woolsey's, Elderflower Tea Shop was my favorite of the Harrington Street shops. Where most of the shop windows were flat, theirs bowed. As the tea shop was twice the size of most of the shops, there were two bulging bow windows that looked like very surprised eyes. The tables in the window enclosures were the best.

Inside, the décor was like something out of Alice in Wonderland. All the tables had lace cloths, though there were round glass tops over them to keep the laundry down. The ceiling was beamed, the wallpaper chintz, and antique dressers and cabinets held assorted tea pots and cups, many of them antique.

When I arrived, both sisters were in the shop. They weren't twins, but they'd worked together and lived together so long that they closely resembled each other.

They wore their hair the same, wore chintz aprons over sensible clothes, and both faces bore the same wrinkled kindness.

Florence saw me, wiped her floury hands on her apron and came toward me with both hands held out. They were as soft and warm as fresh baking as she clutched my own hands. "I am so very sorry for your loss. Agnes was the most wonderful woman, and a good friend. I still can't believe she's gone."

"Thank you, Miss Watt. Neither can I."

"What a shock for you. We wanted to tell you, but no one knew where you or your parents were. We left a message on your parents' home phone. It was the best we could do." She raised her hands as though to say, 'and that was a waste of long distance money.' "Let me get you some tea."

One of the things I loved about Gran and her friends was that they offered tea as though it could cure everything from grief to lovesickness to stress. It might not be a cure, but I knew I'd feel better for the tea and the kindness that went with it.

Florence led me to a table in a quiet corner. Both window tables were taken. One by tourists consulting a guide book as they drank their tea, the other by a table of international students all studiously speaking in English. I connected to the Wi-Fi and checked my email. Of course, there wasn't anything from my mother yet, it was too soon, but I did have an email from my friend Jennifer full of gossip from home.

Jenn always emailed as though she was having an

actual conversation. "Guess what???" she had typed, then left a blank space, presumably so I could either make a few wild guesses or say, "I give up," and read on.

"Toad is single again!!!!" Jenn also loved the exclamation mark the way some people love Margaritas or chocolate. "Word is Monica dumped him!!! Can you believe it???!!"

Another space for me to fill in my answer. Heck, yeah, I could believe it. Any woman with a couple of functioning brain cells could see through Todd the Toad.

Which let me out. I'd stayed with him for two years.

But I was free now. Free. Jennifer suggested we go on a single girls' road trip!!!! To New York!!!! when I got home. I wondered when that would be now that I had a knitting shop on my hands.

Florence Watt brought my tea herself, and I ordered a cheese and pickle sandwich as an early dinner. She didn't stop to visit, because they were busy, which suited me fine. I was glad to be around people but also happy to be left alone while I checked out my late-night visitor. He'd said he lived locally. I wondered if Florence and Mary knew him. I'd have to ask them when they got a second.

Even though I had his website address, I did a search of his name first. He came up right away on the Bodleian Library site. I recognized him in the photograph. He was giving a lecture on book restoration. According to the introduction to his talk, he was an expert in restoration and a dealer in rare books and manuscripts.

His website told me very little that I hadn't already found. He didn't have a storefront, but he was your go-to-guy if you wanted that Dickens first edition you found behind the fireplace valued, or if you wanted to find a particular item, or have an ancient book or manuscript restored.

There were a few scholarly articles linked on the website, with some technical information on restoration, a couple of stories of how he'd been able to track down a rare book for a client, and one about how he'd donated a rare medieval illuminated manuscript to the Bodleian's collection. He also lectured from time to time at King's College.

Impressive credentials. What was missing on his website and, indeed, from all his biographical material, was any hint of, well, his biography. No birthdate, no mention of wife or children. Not that I cared how old he was, if he was married or had kids, it just seemed strange not to have any personal information.

Even if he was an expert on ancient books who lectured at fancy colleges, I'd make sure all the lights were on in the shop this evening, and try and keep the conversation short.

I was relieved to find that Florence and Mary knew Rafe Crosyer, and they confirmed that he was Gran's friend.

Back at the shop, I went back to work tidying and organizing while I continued the inventory. It was tiring, ticklish work and I felt hot and frazzled when Rafe Crosyer knocked on the door.

He, on the other hand, looked as rested as though he'd spent the day sleeping peacefully and had just woken. This made me cranky.

Rafe looked at me searchingly through those piercing blue eyes of his. "I'm so sorry about your grandmother. I only heard today that she's gone. She was a good friend to me. And what a tragedy for you. You look tired."

I'd fought tears many times since I'd found out Gran was dead, but he sounded so sincere I felt my eyes misting. "It was a shock," I admitted. Then, in a low voice, because it was all I could manage. "I'll miss her."

"So will I."

"By the way, if you have a key to the shop, I'd appreciate it if you'd give it to me. Now that Gran's gone, I need to get all the keys in. Her lawyer suggested it." Her lawyer had suggested no such thing but I liked the idea of making the hapless Mr. Tate responsible for me asking the intimidating Rafe Crosyer for his key.

He only raised his eyebrows. "I don't have a key. I told you. Last night when I arrived, the door was unlocked."

I wasn't going to argue with him. What was the point? Instead I decided to get the locks changed.

He glanced around the shop, his eyes resting on the door that led upstairs, but if it was a hint to invite him upstairs, I chose to ignore it. There was only one visitor's chair in the shop itself. I wasn't going to take him to the back room where Gran ran her knitting classes, so we stood there looking at each other.

He said, "I wish I'd been here. I'd have liked to attend the service. If it's not too painful for you, can you tell me what happened?"

Of course it was painful, but I was also glad to talk to someone who'd known my grandmother. "I wish I knew. When I arrived yesterday, there was a notice on the door saying the shop was closed until further notice. It was Miss Watt in the tea shop who told me Gran had passed away. She'd been gone three weeks." I swallowed down the lump in my throat. "I never got the news. I came straight from a dig site in Egypt, where my parents are working. My mother still doesn't know." I shook my head. "It was such a shock."

"To me, too. She seemed perfectly healthy the last time I saw her." He ended the sentence with an upward lilt to his voice, making the statement a question.

"I thought she was healthy, too. It seems she died in her sleep. I missed her funeral as well." I blinked my eyes rapidly and turned my head away, determined this man would not see me cry.

He shifted, no doubt uncomfortable at the thought a woman might cry in front of him. "We can't talk here. Why don't you let me buy you a drink?"

I was about to say no, but then I thought how much I'd like to get away from the shop at night. It felt creepy, especially since I'd found the broken glasses, the bloodstains, and the wool all messed up.

If he really was a friend of Gran's, I wanted to trust

him.

I'd spent too long in my own head today. It would be nice to mingle with people. We'd be able to reminisce about Gran. Get some kind of closure. As though he'd read my mind, he said, "We both missed her funeral. We'll call it a wake."

"All right."

He waited while I took care to close up the shop, double-checking that the door was securely locked. It was just after seven and dusk as we crossed Cornmarket and headed up Ship Street to Turl. He asked politely how I'd enjoyed my time in Egypt as we headed for some of the oldest colleges in Oxford. Turning left on Turl, we passed Exeter College, then hit Broad Street where Trinity and Balliol managed to remain stately and detached behind gates and walls while cars, delivery vans and tourists from around the world thronged the street in front.

I loved this part of Oxford. I liked that these working colleges allowed visitors to walk their beautiful gardens and view the ancient monuments and hear about their history while smart, pimply-faced kids attended classes in the same buildings where Sir Walter Raleigh, Oscar Wilde and Helen Fielding had gone before them.

I told him about the heat of Egypt and a bit about my parents' work. He asked intelligent questions and seemed to know more about their work than I did.

We passed the round Sheldonian theater, designed by Christopher Wren in the 1600s and so bombarded with car exhaust and pollution that it's original golden stone is like an old sepia photograph, the Bodleian's beside it and I remembered that my companion lectured there. "Did you go to Oxford?" I asked him.

"No. Cambridge. But it was a long time ago," and then he asked me about Boston, changing the subject before I could find out more.

When we walked under Oxford's Bridge of Sighs and into a narrow, twisting, alley, I knew we were headed for The Turf, a pub that's been serving beer in Oxford since the Middle Ages. The pub was bright, noisy and busy, with students, tourists and regular locals all mixed up together. I followed him in and he walked straight past the first bar and the crowd around it, into a quieter room. We found a small table tucked in an alcove against a wall, perfect for private conversation. "What can I get you?" he asked.

"What would Gran have had?" I asked him. It was a test. If he knew her well, he'd know her favorite drink. He didn't hesitate, "Harvey's Bristol Cream."

I nodded. He'd passed the test. "That's what I'll have."

When he returned he held two glasses of rich, amber sherry and passed me one. "To Agnes," he said. I'd expected more, a short speech, perhaps, about my grandmother, but, after a pause as though unsure what he should say, Rafe Crosyer merely lifted his glass and sipped. I followed suit. Harvey's Bristol Cream is a very sweet sherry. Even as the intense sweetness filled my mouth, I noticed Rafe start slightly and an expression of distaste flitted across his handsome face.

"You don't like sweet sherry?" I had to ask. In my experience, only old ladies drank it.

"I prefer something stronger," he admitted. "But I wanted to honor your grandmother."

"I can't believe she's gone." Everywhere I looked, I felt as though I'd see her if I looked hard enough. She'd always been here, someone to talk to when my parents were too busy, the beloved grandmother who'd tried and tried to teach me to knit.

I sipped more sherry. "I thought I saw Gran, when I first got here. She was walking along the street, and I was so excited to see her I went running after her, but she turned down a side street and when I got there, she was gone."

He looked at me with sympathy. "Grief hits in surprising ways. Denying the loved one is gone is the first stage."

"But I wasn't grieving then. I didn't even know she was dead."

When he shifted, his legs brushed mine under the table. "On some level, perhaps you did."

Maybe he meant it as a platitude, but his words made me twitchy. "You mean, I'm psychic? Or that was her ghost come to visit?" I didn't like either possibility.

He leaned in and quoted, "There are more things in heaven and earth, Horatio, than are dreamt of in your philosophy."

That's the thing about Oxford. You go for a drink in a pub with some guy and next thing he's quoting Hamlet.

I'd been brought up by a pair of down-to-earth scientists who frowned on anything that smacked of the supernatural. "My philosophy is dust to dust and ashes to ashes."

He seemed as though he was going to say something, and then changed his mind. "What are your plans now?"

I hadn't intended to discuss Gran's will, not with him or anyone, before I'd even spoken to my parents, but he had a way of looking at me that was so understanding that I found myself telling him that Gran wanted me to keep the shop and run it.

He nodded, looking sympathetic, as though he read my ambivalence. I'd never experienced a man listening to me with such complete attention. His blue gaze was intent and not even when a drunk undergrad bumped into the back of his chair and mumbled a slurred, "Sorry, mate," did his gaze waver from mine.

When I'd finished he said, "And will you do it? Will you stay?"

This was the question I'd been wrestling with since I'd left Mr. Tate's office. I lifted my hand to my mouth and gnawed on my thumbnail, a habit I had when I was perturbed. He watched me, his gaze on my mouth, until I caught myself and hastily put my hand back in my lap. "I don't know. I want to respect Gran's last wishes, obviously, but I'm twenty-seven years old. That seems a little young to be running a knitting shop, don't you think?"

He shrugged his broad shoulders as though he'd

never given the age of knitting shop proprietors much thought.

"Anyway, I don't even know how to knit."

"Really? Did your grandmother never teach you?"

I sipped more of the sweet wine. "She tried. I have absolutely no aptitude."

"Perhaps you simply need to practice."

"That's what Gran always said. I'm too impatient. If you'd ever tried knitting, you'd understand."

"I can knit," he said.

Okay, that surprised me so much I choked on a sip of sherry. "Seriously?" It was like hearing that a boxing champion raised orchids as a hobby. It probably happened, but it seemed incongruous. The thought of this dark and virile stranger—who reminded me of a Brontë hero—knitting, well, you never thought of Heathcliff or Mr. Rochester dropping a stitch.

"I believe I mentioned my insomnia." He raised his hands, palms up, "Knitting relaxes me."

It occurred to me that with his cold hands and poor circulation he probably wore a lot of sweaters and scarves. "Well, I don't find getting tangled up in wool relaxing, and I'm not sure I want to stay in Oxford and run a knitting shop." I sighed and my thumb crept toward my mouth again. "Not that I have a lot of other ideas for my future."

"You don't have a job back at home? Or a boyfriend?" He seemed more interested in the second question than the first it seemed to me. Though why would this incredibly sexy, sophisticated man be interested in me? I was the girl-next-door type, a solid B student, and he was the kind of sexy academic who probably dated brilliant supermodels.

"No. My job at home was downsized, and I recently ended a relationship." I left it there. Let him believe that I'd regretfully ended a love affair with a wonderful man, not that I'd been cheated on by The Toad.

"How about you? Do you have, um, a job?" The second the words were out, I realized how stupid I sounded. Of course he had a job, I'd looked at his website. What I really wanted to know was the girlfriend or wife thing, but I didn't want to appear as interested as I was. I quickly added, "I mean, I looked at your website today. Your work sounds so interesting." *Oh, great, now I was gushing. And inane.*

"Evaluating old books is fascinating. I've worked with illuminated manuscripts from Roman times, papyrus scrolls, letters and diaries of the famous and infamous. The actual repair and restoration can be as tedious as you seem to find knitting." When he teased me those winter-blue eyes warmed. "In fact, that's what I wanted to see your grandmother about. An old book."

He was looking at me intently, but then he always looked at me intently; perhaps there was something even more piercing in his gaze, as though I might know what he was talking about. I didn't. "What book?"

"She described it as quite ancient and in need of restoration to preserve it. I believe it's some sort of a record of your family."

Immediately, I knew what he was talking about.

51

"You mean the old family diary?" The one Gran had mentioned in my letter.

"Family diary?"

"That's what she called it. Strange term, since a diary usually belongs to one person, but Gran said that's what made the book so special. Different people had been adding their stories to the book for a long time. She showed it to me once, but I didn't understand it. Some of it was in Latin and some of the writing was so old-fashioned and faded I couldn't make heads or tails of it. There were some very nice drawings, though. We had some good artists in our family."

It came to me, now, almost as though the book was in front of me. It book was bound in leather, badly cracked in places. I could imagine that my grandmother might want it restored, to make sure none of our family history was lost. "She kept it in a glass-fronted bookcase, in the flat. I can show it to you if you like."

"I'd like that very much. I'd be happy to restore it, in your grandmother's honor. I wouldn't charge you for my services."

"That's very generous of you." However, I knew I wouldn't give him the book tonight. Now that I'd been reminded of the family history, I wondered if Gran had added anything to it. I wanted to look at my family history again, hold the book in my hands that I'd seen her with so often. I'd take pictures of all the pages with my phone, just so I'd have a record, before I let a piece of my family history out of my hands.

"Would you like another drink?" he asked politely. I

knew enough about British pub culture to know that this was my round. I said, "Would you?"

His eyes twinkled attractively when he smiled.. "You've yawned twice in the last five minutes. I think if you have another drink, you'll fall asleep at the table."

I put a hand over my mouth to stifle another yawn. "I didn't get much sleep last night." Partly thanks to him coming into the shop in the wee hours. Then, twice last night I'd woken, thinking she was standing at the bottom of my bed. "It's been such a shock."

"Come on, then. Let's get you home."

As we got up to leave, I saw the goth girl I'd seen yesterday when I first arrived in Oxford. I probably wouldn't have noticed her if she hadn't seen us and ducked behind the young guy she was with. Unfortunately, when she did, she bumped into a waitress carrying a tray of food and sent a plate of fish and chips crashing to the ground.

Goth girl walked away as though the disaster was nothing to do with her, but Rafe stepped into her path. "You're not old enough to drink," he said in a warning tone.

She glared at him. "Yes, I am. I just don't look my age." She sounded like a whiny teen, and she sure looked like a whiny teen. I was willing to bet she was lying her pouty face off.

"Go home," Rafe said, "Before you get into trouble."

He was old enough to be her father but I hadn't pictured him having kids, somehow. They glared at each other. Cold blue eyes to hot brown ones. There was never any contest. Within ten seconds she was dropping her gaze and turning away. I don't know what she said to her guy, but he followed her as she stalked out of the pub.

I didn't ask, but my curiosity was so rampant Rafe could probably see it. He said, "She's the daughter of a friend of mine. She's at a difficult age."

I felt a stab of sympathy for the girl. "When you're that age it seems as though you'll never be old enough for all the adult privileges and the teenage years will last for all eternity."

"For Hester, they may."

I laughed. "Do you have children of your own?"

He looked down his nose at me. "Not that I'm aware of." *Spoken like a Regency rake.*

We left the pub. The streets felt utterly silent and empty after the noise and bustle. I've never believed in time travel, but when you walk around Oxford late at night, you are walking through history. Except, of course, for the cars parked on the side of the road and a food truck sitting alone outside the Sheldonian selling kebabs.

The air was crisp, the night clear, and apart from our footsteps the only sound was an owl letting out a haunting cry as it circled, no doubt looking for some unlucky mouse.

When we reached Cardinal Woolsey's, I saw something move in the shadows. I jumped, then the shadow resolved itself into the shape of a black cat. No, not a cat. A kitten, with a skinny body so I worried that it had no home. Its green eyes glowed as the moonlight caught them and it took a dainty step toward me. I wanted to check for a collar and make sure the poor thing wasn't homeless, but when Rafe came up beside me the cat melted back into the darkness.

Before I unlocked the door, I turned to Rafe. "Thank you for the drink. I'm going to bed now. Why don't you come back tomorrow to look at the book?"

I thought he would argue, and then, obviously seeing that I had no intention of letting him inside, he said, "Of course. Perhaps tomorrow evening?"

"That would be fine."

He looked down at me and for a crazy moment I thought he was going to kiss me. The moment stretched. He said, "I hope you decide to stay."

FIVE

BEFORE I COULD decide how to answer, or even what he meant by those cryptic words, he had turned and was walking away down the street.

I let myself in and just for a second I wished that I had invited Rafe inside. I wondered how long it would take until the urge to call out for my grandmother faded. I wondered if I would stay here long enough to find out.

After making sure that the door was securely locked behind me, I went upstairs to the flat. I was glad that Rafe had reminded me of our family book. As tired as I was, I knew I wouldn't sleep until I had looked through it to see if Gran had added her own chapter to our story. Knowing how much she loved history, I suspected she had. I went straight into the living room, switched on lamps, and knelt in front of the glass-fronted bookcase where she'd kept her treasured books. As far as I knew, the family diary had been there forever. Certainly as long as I had been coming here. Gran loved books, and her house was filled with everything from the classics to knitting books to popular paperbacks, but the special ones were in this cabinet.

There was the family Bible, an early, illustrated collection of Dickens's complete works, obscure books of various sizes and antiquity, and some old tomes on folklore and herbs. I'd never really studied the books. They'd just always filled the cabinet. If she hadn't made a point of showing me that family diary, I probably wouldn't have known it was there. I opened the bookcase. The key was in the lock as always and I turned it carefully and opened the glass doors. The book wasn't in the spot where I'd remembered it, the top row towards the right-hand side.

I carefully looked at the titles one by one. Our family history wasn't there. I looked again, more slowly this time, pulling out any book that appeared remotely similar to the one I remembered, but still, I didn't find the book. I closed the cabinet at last, feeling puzzled. Gran wasn't the sort to leave a book that was both precious and fragile out somewhere. If she'd been reading it, she'd have marked her place with a bookmark and returned the book to its spot. Well, she must've moved the book to a new home, and now I would have to find it.

I yawned so wide my jaw cracked. The sleepless night, and that glass of sherry, were catching up with me. I would search properly for that book in the morning.

I was barely settled in bed, and beginning to float in that twilight between being completely awake and completely asleep when I heard something at my window. No doubt it was the wind, or the old place settling for the night. I turned on my side facing the wall and ignored it.

The sound came again, like someone tapping on the window. A shiver of fear ran over my skin and my eyes popped open wide. I cursed every horror movie I had ever seen, and the entire works of Stephen King, as I reached out and turned on the lamp on my bedside table. I picked up my cell phone, but I felt a little foolish calling 999 to report unidentified tapping on the window. I would have to investigate.

The floor felt cold under my bare feet. I clutched my phone ready to call for help as I edged closer to the window. When I heard a pathetic and plaintive meow, the fear was immediately washed away by relief. I recognized the black cat. It was the same one that had been hanging around outside the shop's front door. It stared at me through the dark glass and meowed again. I opened the window and the cat stepped inside and onto the windowsill.

"Well, look at you," I said, putting out my hand to stroke the silky fur. The cat arched its back against my palm and began to purr immediately. To be honest, I was delighted to have another living thing in the house. "You're so skinny. Doesn't anyone feed you?"

By way of answer, the cat meowed again, jumped down onto the floor and circled, its furry body brushing my legs. I leaned down to check but there was no collar.

"You know, in Egypt, they worship the cat. You should go there, you'd have a better life."

Having spent more time at digs in Egypt and the Sudan than I'd spent at summer camp meant I was full of strange facts about the past. "Bastet, that's the name of the cat goddess. Bastet," I said. "Is that your name?"

You have to remember how completely sleep deprived I was, and forgive me for this inane conversation I was having with a kitten. Did I really think it was going to answer me? It gave me a look as though thinking it had chosen the wrong window.

I didn't know much about cats, but I had a strong feeling that this one was hungry. And yes, I asked if it was hungry and would like some milk, and the cat meowed. I picked it up and the small, warm body curled comfortably against my chest as we walked downstairs and into the kitchen. I poured a dish of milk into one of the flowered china bowls and placed it on the floor. I didn't want to think of the tiny creature as 'it' so I played with names.

The kitten sat, curled her tail around herself and began to lap at the milk. I wasn't completely sure the kitten was a her, not wanting to pry, but I thought it was female.

As I looked at her shiny black fur and thought of her being out in the night, I recalled the story about Nyx, the daughter of Chaos, and goddess of night. "Nyx," I said aloud, and I could have sworn the kitten gave a nod of approval. I pronounced her name to rhyme with tricks as she seemed like a tiny trickster.

I hadn't done much in the way of grocery shopping, and I didn't see anything in the fridge that would appeal to a cat. When I searched through the food cupboard I found a tin of lobster pâté, which I opened and put on a plate. The cat made short work of the lobster pâté, then finished the milk, and looked at me as though waiting for the next item on the agenda.

It was too late to try and find the owner, and I didn't want to send the small creature back out into the night. I remembered that owl circling the area, hunting, and decided to let my new friend stay if it wanted to. I went back to the bedroom and Nyx followed me.

I opened the window wide enough that she could leave if she wanted to and then got back into bed. She stared at me, blinked, and then jumped up onto the bed. She curled up beside me and immediately went to sleep. I switched out the light and settled myself. It was nice having the cat curled up, warm against my side, and purring softly. I had the feeling that neither of us wanted to be alone tonight. It was my last thought before I fell into a deep sleep.

I woke suddenly without knowing what had woken me. Was it a dream? I had a sense of darkness, and someone had screamed, but I couldn't capture the dream. Or was it a noise that had woken me? I blinked against the darkness. I've read many times that if you wake in the night and want to get back to sleep, it's best not to look at the time. I looked anyway. It was three in the morning. I calculated I'd slept about four hours. I tried to settle myself once more for sleep but a small, furry head butted itself against my shoulder. I reached out to pat the kitten but it evaded my hand and kept butting me. Maybe she wanted to go out. I didn't know that much about cats, but I had left the window open, and assumed that if the kitten could climb up from the street and tap on my window, then she could walk back out again. But, it seemed the cat had other ideas. "All right," I said at last and reached out to turn on the lamp.

The cat led me straight to the kitchen, and when I'd poured her a saucer of milk, she lapped the milk greedily. "I hope you're a good mouser. And just so we start off on the right foot, don't think you need to leave me dead rodents as gifts. I'll take your purring as thanks."

She lifted her head, looked at me, and burped.

SIX

I AWOKE THE next morning feeling much better. The heavy weight of grief still pressed upon my chest, but it's amazing what a solid night of sleep will do for a person's perspective. The kitten was still in my bed and rolled around playfully when I stroked her belly. I knew I was going to have to start searching for her real owner, but given how skinny she was, I wasn't in a big hurry. This morning I decided I would find that book, try to track down my parents again by telephone, and make some definite decisions about what I was going to do with this shop, and my future.

I put on a pair of the purple and green hand-knit socks I found in the top drawer of the bureau in my room, wrapped myself in my robe, and padded down to the kitchen. I made myself coffee and toast, and Nyx enjoyed a dish of deviled crab which had lain hidden in the back of the cupboard. I suspected it and the lobster pâté had been part of a gift basket. There were no other cans that were likely to tempt Nyx, though, so I decided to visit the Full Stop.

After showering and dressing in my best jeans and a black sweater, I wrote a note saying that if anyone was missing a small black kitten, they should call my mobile. Full Stop had a community board, where I could pin my notice, and no doubt the Watt sisters would display one too.

This reminded me that I hadn't changed over to a UK plan for my phone, so I did that first. I dithered for a second over which plan to take. I usually go with a one month pay-as-you-go, but if I was staying, I should get a proper plan. Was I staying? I was still far from certain, so I stuck with my usual temporary plan and put the number on my homemade flyers.

The cat regarded me with its head tipped to one side, as though she was considering whether she wanted to stay with me or not. She was so adorable I laughed. Her green-gold eyes seemed to glow and I thought I'd angered her. I shook my head. How foolish I was acting over a kitten.

There was a good chance that someone in the neighborhood would recognize the cat so, I decided to take her with me. Nyx seemed quite amenable to this idea and when I repurposed one of the wicker baskets that we used to store wool and placed a folded towel into the bottom, she quite happily jumped in.

We made the short stroll up to the grocer's. An older gentleman was running the cash register. I politely made my request, and if he looked slightly askance at a cat in his food store, he was too polite to throw us out. I find people in the UK are much more tolerant of animals in shops than I'm used to in the States.

On the community board were such delightful announcements as that private tutoring was available in Latin, bell ringers were wanted at one of the churches (previous experience helpful) and someone had a pianoforte for sale. Who knew pianofortes were so expensive? Someone was looking for accommodation, and someone else was offering a room in a house. It seemed those two should talk.

There was no note, however, asking for the return of a small black cat. I pinned my own notice up in a prominent spot and then began to collect a few items to purchase.

There weren't many options in the cat food department. When I held the basket up and showed Nyx the choices, she turned her body all the way around as though she wouldn't lower herself to look at canned cat food. I'd have thought this was a coincidence except that I noticed her tiny paw stretched out behind me and when I turned I was standing in front of a selection of tinned fish.

Surely not. A tiny kitten couldn't possibly recognize canned seafood, could she? I stepped closer and held the basket up. Nyx stretched out her paw and touched the cans of tuna. I put three in the basket and then, thinking that that a steady diet of tuna might be dull, offered her such options as salmon—sockeye or pink—mackerel, oysters, and sardines. Her paw remained inside the basket.

"Okay," I said. "Tuna it is."

For myself, I picked up some eggs, a block of cheese, a fresh loaf of bread, and a packet of tea. I was about to reach for a bottle of milk when I nearly collided with a man bent on the same task. "After you," he said, drawing back and allowing me first choice of the milk on display. If I was a cat, I'd have purred. He had fair, wavy hair, humorous-looking green eyes and the kind of skin that freckles in the sun. He wasn't much taller than me, but he looked like he worked out. He wore black trousers, a white shirt and a tie loosened at the neck.

I had a momentary impression that he'd seen and done things he'd rather not have. I didn't want to stand in the middle of the small shop and stare, though he was definitely stare-worthy, so I thanked him, helped myself to a pint of semi-skim and went to the front counter to pay.

While the older gentleman rang up my purchases, I said, "I'm wondering if you recognize this cat. She seems to be a stray."

The man did not appear to be a cat lover. He gave the briefest of glances into the basket and shook his head, disapprovingly, I thought. "No. Haven't seen it before."

The hottie who'd almost bumped into me over the milk lined up behind me, holding a chocolate bar and a ready-made sandwich along with his milk. The man behind the register jutted his chin at him. "You'd best ask him. He's a policeman. They know about missing persons."

He raised his eyebrows. "Missing persons?"

I smiled perfunctorily. "He's joking. This cat appears to have mislaid its owner."

He looked from the cat to me. "Or found a new one."

"I'm not sure I want a cat. I'm not even sure I'm staying."

"You're American," he said. "Attending one of the colleges?"

I shook my head. "I can't even imagine being smart enough to go to one of the Oxford colleges. Do you go to college here?"

"Mr. Teasdale was correct. I'm a local police officer."

I nodded. "I'd guessed military."

I paid for my groceries and, with a nod, left the store. I hadn't gone far when the police officer caught up with me. I was flattered before I realized that he was about to pass me, and was simply a quicker walker than I was. Before he got more than a step ahead of me I said, "Could I ask you something?"

He turned. "Of course."

I couldn't stop thinking about Gran's broken glasses, those few spots of what I thought were blood on the floor, and signs that her shop had been rapidly tidied up by someone who didn't know where things belonged. There were so many things I didn't understand. "My grandmother died a few weeks ago."

"I'm very sorry to hear it."

"Thank you. The thing is, I wasn't here, and all I know is that she apparently died in her sleep. I don't even know what was wrong with her. Would there be some kind of coroner's report?"

He looked at me curiously. "You'll want to ask your grandmother's doctor for that information. It wouldn't be a police matter." He kept his gaze on my face and I had the feeling that he could see inside my head to the worries I had about those broken glasses.

I tried my best to look inscrutable but I don't think I succeeded very well.

"Do you think your grandmother's death might benefit from further investigation?"

Honestly, I had no idea. Gran could have broken her glasses and bought new ones. But, then, where were the new ones? I didn't have anything more than a hunch that Gran's death wasn't as straightforward as I'd been told. "I'll feel better once I've spoken to her doctor."

Of course, being a woman who prided herself on never getting sick, Gran didn't have a regular doctor. I had no idea who'd even signed her death certificate.

He nodded and then pulled a business card from his pocket. "If you want to talk about anything, give me a ring."

I read aloud from his business card, "Detective Inspector Ian Chisholm." Now I understood why he wasn't in uniform. "I really appreciate this."

"All part of the service." His smile was his nicest feature, I discovered, when he treated me to it. Warm, intimate and sexy. Was he flirting? After Toad I had so little faith in men, or in myself, that I couldn't believe a normal, attractive man might be showing interest in me.

"And you are?"

I giggled, foolishly. "I'm Lucy. My grandmother ran Cardinal Woolsey's just down the street."

He slowed his pace and we walked together towards the wool shop, Nyx watching from her basket. "I met your grandmother. I went into Cardinal Woolsey's to buy a gift for my auntie. She's a champion knitter. Your grandmother helped me choose a pattern and some wool, and, as far as I could tell, Auntie was pleased with my gift."

"That's nice. Gran was so well known, and did such a wonderful job with the store."

"Be a shame to see it go. You live in a place like Oxford and think nothing ever changes, but of course it does."

"Gran wanted me to take over the shop." I don't know what made me blurt that out. Perhaps, because I had no one to talk to about my dilemma.

He looked startled. "Aren't you a bit young for a knitting shop?"

I was pleased he thought so. "Worse, I can't even knit. I loved my grandmother, though, and the shop meant everything to her. I'm very torn."

"Well, don't do anything in haste." We'd arrived at a somewhat old and battered Mini Cooper. "This is me. As I said, feel free to call me. Anytime." And, with a final nod, he opened the door and climbed in. I kept walking, thinking I'd met two men in the last couple of days who were more interesting than any I'd met in the last few years.

I unlocked the door and entered Cardinal Woolsey's. I suppose, had I not been thinking about my recent encounter with the dishy detective, I would have been a bit more perceptive to clues that something strange was going on under my nose.

I closed the door behind me, locking it carefully, then placed the basket on the floor so the cat could jump out. I was about to head upstairs when I noticed a woman standing looking at the baskets of wool.

Her back was to me. She was an older woman with pure white hair, wearing a flowered skirt, a black hand-knit cardigan, and sensible black shoes. I felt a pang of sadness seeing how very much she looked like my grandmother from the back.

But what on earth was she was doing here? How did she get in? I was about to question her when, as though she felt my presence, the woman turned.

If I'd still been carrying the basket, I'd have dropped it, cat and all. As it was, my hand flew to my mouth. I backed up until I banged into the door, staring.

The woman in the shop *was* my grandmother. Not someone who looked like her, it really *was* her. "Gran?" I asked, my voice shaking as I stared, fear warring with hope.

She reached toward me, and her face lit with her beautiful smile. "Lucy. My dear, I thought I'd never see you again."

I rushed forward, feeling tears start to my eyes. When I gripped her hands they were so cold. "Gran. Where have you been? What happened? I don't understand."

She looked at me and a puzzled expression crossed her face. "I don't understand, either, though I feel very peculiar." She glanced around. "And why is the shop so out of order?"

I rubbed my hands up her arms trying to warm her. Her face was pale, her eyes searching my face. "Gran, you don't have your glasses on. You can't see without them."

She put a hand to her face and blinked as though she was only now noticing that she wasn't wearing her glasses. "Isn't that a funny thing? I see you perfectly well."

"I'm so confused. Miss Watt said you were..." I couldn't finish the sentence. I couldn't say the word dead, so I substituted 'gone.'

"Gone? Where would I have gone? I've been so looking forward to your visit."

As happy as I was to see her, something was terribly wrong. "Did you have some kind of accident? I found your glasses, and they were broken, and I think there was blood on the floor."

She looked around the shop. "I don't remember. It's all so fuzzy. The last thing I recall, I was here, working as usual. Someone came in..." She searched the shop again as though she could bring back her memory by actually looking for it. As her gaze moved around the shelves she said, "What's the Cashmere Tweed doing where the Cotton Cashmere should be?"

I was about to suggest we go upstairs for a proper

chat when I heard noises coming from the back room where Gran offered knitting classes. A woman peered cautiously from behind the curtain and then, seeing the two of us, walked in. I recognized her immediately. She was the woman I'd seen with Gran the day I arrived.

She looked like Helen Mirren, very glamorous in a way that embraced her older years. Her silver hair was stylish, her make-up perfect and she wore the most beautiful hand-knit dress in an intricate pattern. It was wearable art all done in soft greens that matched the faded moss color of her eyes. She also looked annoyed. Her lips were pursed and she said, quite sharply, "Agnes! What are you doing up here?"

My grandmother turned to look at her. "Why Sylvia. Are you early for the meeting?"

The woman shifted her gaze to me. She smiled, a cold smile. "The shop is closed until further notice, I'm afraid. Perhaps you can see yourself out?"

Obviously, I didn't show myself out. I said, "I'm Agnes's granddaughter, Lucy." My mind was jumbling with questions. Strangely, the one that came to the fore was that yet another strange person was wandering about the shop. She'd appeared from the back room, soundlessly. "How did you get in here?"

Her lips folded even tighter. "Oh dear, this is rather a pickle. I have to speak to Rafe," she said almost to herself. "He'll know what to do."

She seemed to think that she was in charge, when the shop belonged to Gran. I wondered how many men in Oxford were called Rafe. "Do you mean Rafe

Crosyer?"

Her eyes widened. "You know Rafe?"

"Not well. But we've met."

"Did he explain to you about your grandmother?"

"Explain what?" As I recalled, he'd asked me for information about her death. But there were those strange clues that maybe Gran hadn't been quite right in her head recently. Had she been put in a home or something? But why say that she was dead?

She ignored my question, shaking her head. "He might not know Agnes is dead. He's been away." She gave a tiny gasp and her gaze darted towards me. I felt like saying, "Yep, outside voice." But I didn't. I was too shocked. What did this woman mean that my grandmother was dead? She was standing right in front of us, looking as puzzled as I felt.

Was this glamorous older woman a crazy person? Had she been holding my grandmother hostage? Had the two of them escaped from a dementia home? My mind was in such a turmoil I wondered if I had fallen asleep and not noticed. Finally, after we both stared at each other for a good twenty seconds, the woman who called herself Sylvia said, "Agnes and I are going to go in the back of the store for a little while. Rafe will know what to do."

I shook my head. I'm not a very brave person, but my grandmother looked frail and confused and I love her as much as I love anyone in the world. I was not letting her out of my sight. "Wait. I'm calling him right now."

"Rafe? You can't call him now."

It was the middle of the afternoon on a Wednesday. I couldn't imagine why not. I told the very bossy Helen Mirren look-alike that Rafe had told me I could call him night or day.

I got my wallet. Instead of pulling out Rafe's business card, I chose DI Ian Chisholm's. Let this woman think I was phoning Rafe. It would keep her calm while I called the cops. While I was retrieving my mobile from my bag, Gran and Sylvia spoke quietly in the corner. I have particularly acute hearing, but Gran had obviously forgotten this fact. Her voice was perfectly audible when she sighed and said, "It's so lovely to see Lucy again. I've missed her so much."

Sylvia scolded, "You cannot show yourself to the living. I know you're new at this, but there are rules. Nothing but harm can come to us if we break those rules."

Rules? Did the crazy woman have my grandmother in some kind of cult? My hands fumbled as I punched in the inspector's number. I didn't want to alert the crazy person who seemed to have my grandmother in her power to what I was doing. Luckily, he answered right away, "Ian Chisholm."

"This is Lucy Swift. We met earlier today."

His voice warmed immediately. "I'm delighted to hear from you. How are things at Cardinal Woolsey's?"

"That's why I'm calling you. There's something going on here that's worrying me."

"What is it?" Something in my voice must've

alerted him to the fact that I wasn't calling to flirt or ask for a date. I was full-out terrified and I had no idea what to do.

I licked my lips. "I wonder if you could drop by the store?"

"On my way."

I turned back to the two women still whispering in the corner. I hoped the detective would arrive quickly. I had no idea if Sylvia might be dangerous. Something about her suggested that she could be.

"Was that Rafe?" she asked.

I was about to speak when a deep male voice said, "Did you want me?" And then Rafe walked out from the back of the shop. I blinked, and wondered again if I was dreaming, but my cell phone was still in my hand and when I pinched my arm I felt pain.

He took in the scene at once. "Ah," he said.

Sylvia turned to him, looking annoyed. "Is that the best you can do? Rafe, this is a disaster. I cannot manage Agnes. She was an insomniac in life and she appears to be one in death. I barely get a wink of sleep worrying she'll get out of bed and go wandering. Yesterday she actually went outside in the daylight."

He ignored Sylvia. He was looking at me. And at the phone in my hand. "Whom did you telephone?" he asked. His tone was mild enough, but authoritative. This was a man who was used to having his questions answered promptly and no doubt his orders obeyed. I lifted my chin. "I called the police. I don't understand what's going on here but I think my grandmother is in danger."

Sylvia shrieked. "The police? No. Rafe. Stop her."

Once more, Rafe ignored her. He came closer to me and held my gaze with his. His eyes were serious and, I thought, sincere. "I know this is going to be very hard for you to understand, and there isn't much time. For everyone's sake, I need you to tell the police that you made a mistake. We'll explain everything to you, but if you bring in outsiders you'll put us all in danger."

"In danger of what? I don't understand. First, everyone said my grandmother was dead, and now here she is as large as life, but she doesn't remember anything. Something sinister is going on."

He let out a heavy sigh. "Something terrible did happen here. Look at your grandmother. Look carefully."

Something about his words made a shiver go down my spine. But the closer I was to my grandmother the safer I could keep her so I followed his instructions. When I was very close to her he reached out and lifted her chin. "Look carefully. What do you see? On her neck?"

There were two very clear puncture wounds on Gran's neck. "They look like bite marks." I looked at Gran. "Did a dog bite you?"

It was Rafe who answered. "Not a dog." Even as Sylvia said, "Rafe, no," he spoke over her. "Your grandmother was bitten by a vampire."

SEVEN

MY FIRST IMPULSE was to laugh and so I did. I burst out laughing. Not the humorous *hahaha* of someone who's heard a good joke, but the hysterical laughter of someone who will soon be carted away to a place where the walls are padded.

No one laughed with me, and soon my chuckles subsided. Rafe's eyes never left mine. "I'm sorry. It would've been far better if you had never found out. And, of course, you can never tell anyone."

"Are you serious?" I looked at all three of them. My grandmother didn't seem at all sure, but the other two nodded, looking extremely serious. Now it came back to me how Rafe always had cold hands, and was unavailable to meet during the day. "Are you two—" I couldn't finish the sentence. It was too absurd. But they obviously knew where I was going and they both nodded slowly.

"We mean no harm," Rafe said. "We meet regularly in your shop. Your grandmother has always been very good to us. And now she's one of us."

"You meet in the shop? But what do you do here?"

They looked at me as though I'd said something very stupid. Rafe and Sylvia answered together, "We knit."

I've heard it said that among their other powers, vampires can look at you in a certain way and get you to do their bidding. But that's not why I agreed to keep their secret. I didn't believe for a second that my grandmother was a vampire. I didn't believe in vampires. They were creatures of fiction, not personalities who knitted socks and crept along the dark streets of Oxford. But, on the other hand, his warning felt serious to me. If I brought the police in they would investigate. I didn't know what they would find, but on the wild possibility that it was true and my grandmother were undead, I had to protect her.

Even as I agreed to Rafe's plan, I wondered if I was as crazy as the rest of them. I had no idea. Sometimes you just go on instinct.

Rafe lifted his head. I have acute hearing, but nowhere near as sharp as his. "He's coming. Sylvia, Agnes, we must go."

"Gran!" I hated that she was following them obediently into the back of the shop. She turned, smiled her sweet smile and said, "It's all right, Lucy. Everything's going to be all right."

They headed for the back and I said, "You'd better come back as soon as he's gone. I want a full explanation." Rafe paused in the doorway leading to the back. He turned his head and looked at me. "Don't worry, we'll be back tonight. Our knitting club meets here every Wednesday at ten."

Trust me to find myself in the only shop in the world that ran a vampire knitting club.

* * *

They had barely left the front of the shop when there was a sharp knock on the door. I tried to pull myself together and push the horror of the last few minutes to the back of my mind. I forced a pleasant smile on my face and opened the door. Ian Chisholm stood there. All signs of the cheerful, mildly flirtatious guy were gone. He said, "Lucy? Are you all right? What's going on?"

I shook my head, holding onto the smile even though I wanted to tell him everything. He was so clearly alive and human and warm, but I'd promised and, until I knew more, I didn't dare tell the police this absurd vampire story. "I'm sorry. I've been so foolish. Please, come in."

He entered and glanced rapidly around the shop before shutting the door behind him. He didn't know me very well. I hated for him to think I was the kind of foolish person who calls the police for no reason, but it was the only plan I had, to let him think I was exactly that foolish.

"I heard strange noises here in the shop, and I thought we had a break-in. But I'm such an idiot." I laughed in a slightly hysterical way. "It was the cat. I'm not used to having a cat. Well, in fact, I don't have a cat, as you know, this one seems to be a stray. Anyway, I forgot all about her and then I heard these strange noises and panicked. I thought I'd had a break-in." Nyx, obediently, poked her head out of a basket of wool on one of the shelves.

As though I'd directed her, she jumped from that basket to a higher shelf and, as she did so, her back paws knocked the basket so its contents tumbled to the floor, hitting knitting needles on the way down that landed on the wooden floor with a clatter.

I dashed over and began picking up the needles and pushing them back into the basket. "You see what I mean? I was upstairs and heard all this noise. I knew I'd locked the shop when I came back from the store and I was convinced someone had broken in. I'm so sorry I bothered you."

"It's no bother You can thank me for my time by making me a cup of tea since I had to cut my lunch short."

I couldn't pretend I didn't have tea, since he'd seen me buying it and the milk at the store. I couldn't think of a reason to get rid of him so I decided the easiest thing was to give him his tea and send him on his way. "Of course. The kitchen is in the flat upstairs." I picked up my groceries, opened the door and ushered him through.

He was perfectly pleasant, but I felt that he wasn't, in fact, off duty. It seemed to me, that he was acting very much like a detective, his eyes searching and his brain busy.

I'm no actress at the best of times and I was still in shock, but I did my best to act cool. I made tea and brought it into the living room. We sat side by side on two chintz chairs and he said, " I found out the name of your grandmother's doctor, the one who signed the death certificate."

He must have done it right after he left me, on his lunch break. If I hadn't been so stunned, I'd have been very flattered.

He pulled a notebook from his pocket and opened it. "It's Dr. Weaver. Christopher Weaver. His surgery is off Walton Street."

"That was so kind of you. Thank you."

"As I said earlier, I met your grandmother. She was a nice lady." He smiled at me. "If I'd arrived to find my grandmother had passed away, I'd have questions, too."

Oh he had no idea. I said, "I'm still having trouble accepting that she's gone."

He nodded. "Grief is a funny thing. Of course, you go through the stages of disbelief, denial, bargaining, and finally acceptance. But it's not a smooth path." He had no idea how right he was. I seemed to be stuck in denial. Or Gran was.

He glanced around. "This room seems very like her."

"Yes." Everything from the framed botanical prints to her collection of Victorian dolls with their china faces, her chintz furniture, and the knitting books and magazines in the book shelves proclaimed that this was her home.

"In my line of work I see a number of bereaved people. It's the ones who keep moving forward with their own lives who do better. The grief and heartbreak don't go, but those who recover fastest have something else to occupy their minds."

I nodded. "Well, I've made one decision today. When I arrived here, I had planned to stay for a month or two. I was going to have a holiday, and help my grandmother in the shop. Today I decided that I'm going to reopen and run Cardinal Woolsey's for at least another month or two while I make up my mind about the future." I'd been toying with the idea, but seeing my grandmother, or what was left of her, had made my decision. I wasn't going anywhere until I knew more.

He seemed pleased at my announcement. "That sounds like an excellent plan."

"It feels good to make some kind of decision." I glanced at the wall clock. "If I phone Dr. Weaver right away, he may even be able to see me today."

He took the hint and rose. I stood as well, to see him out, and he held my gaze. His eyes were searching which immediately made me feel hot, as though he could see all the secrets I was trying to hide. "Is anything bothering you? I can be a good listener, you know."

Once more I was conscious of a desire to cast myself onto his broad chest and tell him everything. He had a trustworthy face and nice eyes. I teetered on the brink. Nyx chose that moment to leap off the couch and pounce on my toes. "Ouch!" I cried, laughing as I scooped her up. "She's practicing her mouse catching, I think." The urge to blab passed. "No. There's nothing bothering, particularly. I'm just sad about Gran."

He reached out and patted Nyx, who flirted with him shamelessly, rolling her head so he could scratch under her chin and purring in ecstasy. "I'll be on my way, but do keep in touch."

I nodded. Two hours ago I would have been thrilled at the idea that this man wanted to stay in touch with me. Now that I was already hiding secrets from his all-too perceptive gaze, I wasn't so sure.

As soon as he left, I called Dr. Weaver's office. If anyone could help me figure out what was going on with Gran, whether she was alive, dead, or undead, presumably it would be the doctor who had last examined her.

The call was answered by a recorded message telling me that surgery hours were that evening from seven until ten. I assumed if the hours were advertised on the message, patients must be able to drop in, so I decided to go that evening at seven.

I suspected my brain was disordered by grief, but the vaguest possibility that there were, indeed, vampires who used the shop as their clubhouse, had me determined to protect myself as best I could. I didn't have a stake on hand, but the shop carried wooden knitting needles and, under Nyx's curious gaze, I took a paring knife and sharpened a couple of them.

For practice, I pretended to stab the hearts of the pretty Victorian dolls, who gazed at me reproachfully from round, blue painted eyes.

"What else?" I asked the cat, thinking the knitting needles weren't very sturdy. I might be able to stake a doll, but someone the size of, say, Rafe Crosyer would need a vastly more substantial stake.

Not that I wanted to kill a vampire, only ward it off. I thought of what I knew of vampires, all of which had come from movies and books. I made a list of the things I needed, then dug through my grandmother's cupboards until I found an empty jam jar with a lid.

I put on my coat and headed back to the grocer's, where I bought two net bags filled with garlic. I would have bought strings of the stuff, but the grocer only carried little bags, each containing three large garlic bulbs. Perhaps I could tie them together with some wool and hang them around my neck.

At the top of Harrington, where it crossed New Inn Street was a church. It was made of gray stone and on one side featured a graveyard with headstones so old and weathered that no hint remained of who lay beneath. The jagged stones seemed like wagging fingers scolding me as I entered the cool church with the empty jam jar. A paper notice listed the hymns to be sung at the six o'clock evensong. Another reminded visitors that brass rubbings were not allowed.

Fortunately, the church was deserted at this time of day. My footsteps sounded like dropping pebbles as I headed across the flagstone floor to the baptismal font. I felt the figures in the stained glass windows frowning down at me as I dipped my jar into the font, glad there was no notice actually forbidding the taking of holy water.

I put two pounds into the donation box as a sop to my conscience and walked past the silent, empty wooden pews on my way out.

A tour group walked by and I longed to climb onto one of the huge tour buses that I knew were waiting down side streets to pick up their customers and drive them onto the next stop, Stratford-upon-Avon, Blenheim Palace, or Bicester Village for the shopping.

I didn't come from a Catholic family, so I was short on crucifixes, also silver, since my jewelry tended to be of the costume variety, what little I had. So, when I turned into Harrington Street once more, I stopped at Pennyfarthing Antiques. A bell tinkled as I entered the dim shop, so cluttered with furniture, hanging lamps, standing lamps, chairs, footstools, paintings and china that I stood very still, letting my eyes become accustomed, before moving inside the shop. I'd been inside before, of course, but Mr. and Mrs. Wright, who owned Pennyfarthing, seemed more interested in buying new stock than selling what they had. Each time I visited, the shop was more crowded than the last.

I made my way around a bowfront cabinet absolutely crammed with china. It contained everything from Royal Doulton figurines of ladies in old-fashioned dresses, to salt and pepper shakers shaped like pigs, and porcelain animals in every possible breed of dog, horse, and even a badger. I spotted a black cat with green eyes that resembled Nyx.

I stepped over a dainty needlepoint footstool, thought how much Gran would have liked the china doll sitting on top of a Chippendale chair, threaded my way between an armoire and a bookcase filled with everything from children's books to leather bound Latin primers, and finally emerged at the glass display cases near the sales counter at the back.

Inside, were trays of jewelry, watches, military medals, brooches, assorted crafting tools and small items that were valuable and easy to steal.

Mr. Wright had his back to me, and was polishing something, whistling as he worked.

"Mr. Wright?" I didn't want to say his name too loud and frighten him.

He turned all the way around and I let out a shriek as the deadly-looking sword in his hand swung my way, light glinting off its razor-sharp blade. There was a sound like a bitten fingernail as the sword nicked the button on my coat.

Mr. Wright peered at me and then said, as though he hadn't nearly run me through, "Why it's Agnes's granddaughter. How lovely to see you." Then, obviously remembering the tragedy, said, "We were so sorry to lose your grandmother. She was a wonderful woman. Excellent neighbor."

I thanked him, agreed that she was a wonderful woman and a most beloved grandmother. He seemed to have forgotten he was holding a deadly weapon and I stepped back, out of the immediate death zone. "That's a nice sword." *And get it out of my face.*

He didn't take the hint and put it down, instead, he raised it, so we could both study it. "Nice example of a1790s Prussian field sword." The blade was about two feet long and narrow. "Look at this," he said, pointing to a groove down the center of the blade. "See how it's channeled? That's to make the blood flow out of the victim faster."

"How interesting," I said in a faint voice.

"We just got a new collection in. An estate sale. Come and look." He brought me behind the counter to the table where he'd been working. There were several more swords and daggers lined up awaiting polishing.

"You'll like this one, it's American. An 1864 cavalry dress sword."

"The carving's pretty," I said.

"That one's the oldest," he said, pointing to a much shorter weapon, a knife rather than a sword. "It's a double-bladed dagger from the sixteenth century, I reckon. Lovely piece. Look at the way the cross-guard curves." I assumed he was referring to the bendy thing at the bottom of the handle. I supposed the stabber would rest their grip on it and press hard as they pushed the dagger into the stabbee. At the end of the curve were round steel loops that I assumed were decorative. The handle was covered in leather that had darkened, presumably from the sweat and oil on the hands of those who'd wielded it.

"It looks awfully sharp," I said.

"Oh, yes, my dear, they're beautifully sharp. The collector kept them in perfect order."

As sharp as a vampire's teeth, which reminded me of why I was here. "I'm looking for a sterling silver cross on a silver chain, if you have it. A nice big cross."

"Yes, of course. They're all in here. Let me get the key." He had a collection of keys hanging from a belt loop and, as he fumbled through them, he was still holding the Prussian sword. A male voice said, "Dad, what are you doing, frightening away the customers?"

I turned and from behind a rack of antique clothing, emerged the Wright's son, Peter. The layout of their shop was similar to Gran's and Peter had obviously come from their flat. I wished he'd come five minutes earlier when his father really had frightened me.

There was a clatter like dropped spoons and then Mr. Wright got down on the floor to find his bunch of keys. Peter came up and took the sword from him, giving me a comical look of exaggerated horror. "I'll finish up here, Dad. You go and help Mum upstairs." He turned to me. "How can I help you?"

Peter was in his mid-forties and was in the army. His parents were very proud of him. His years in the desert had left his skin permanently darkened. He wore his hair short and his shirt and trousers were ironed as carefully as a dress uniform. He had two children and I seemed to recall there was trouble in the marriage. Or, maybe, he was divorced. Gran had told me, but I'd forgotten.

His father nodded and then, as his son took his place in front of the glass case, said, "You remember Lucy, from next door?"

"I'm not really from next door, but Agnes Bartlett was my grandmother. I'm visiting."

Peter looked at me searchingly for a few seconds and then said, "I'd hardly have recognized you. You're all grown up." He looked at his dad and added, "And isn't she a beauty?"

"That she is."

"Oh, stop it, you two," I said, laughing. But I was relieved that Peter had put the sword back on the table and had taken over from his father, who headed for the rack of antique clothing and the door to his home.

"I was sorry to hear about your grandmother," Peter said, as he tried several keys for the cabinet until he found the right one.

"Thank you. I still can't believe it."

"Death's like that. Even in a war zone, you never expect it."

"Are you going back?"

"Oh, no. My parents need me. They've gone downhill since I was last here." He shook his head. "The shop's too much for them, now. What this shop needs, what they all need, is some new blood."

There didn't seem to be a tactful answer, so I made one of those sounds that could mean anything. Then I pushed the button that got the trays moving. I went through trays of old rings and brooches, charm bracelets, snuff boxes, pillboxes, watches, necklaces and earrings galore. Among the offerings were a few small silver crosses for little girls on dainty silver chains but that wasn't what I wanted. When I explained that I was looking for something more substantial he said, "Wait a minute, I think there are some bigger items back here. Just a mo."

When he disappeared, I looked in another cabinet that held watches, from gold pocket watches to cheap knock offs. When I finished browsing and raised my head, I noticed a business card sitting on top of the cabinet. Sidney Lafontaine.

Sidney Lafontaine who had a client interested in buying Cardinal Woolsey's.

Had she been in Pennyfarthing's as well? I'd assumed her buyer was interested in a knitting shop, but perhaps any shop on the street would do.

Peter returned with three thick silver chains of varying lengths, and two silver crosses. One of the crosses was about an inch tall and the other twice the size. I chose the larger of the crosses and the thickest of the chains.

After inspecting the Sterling mark on both items, I attached the cross to the chain. It was large enough that I could slip it over my head. I liked the heft of the piece. It cost two hundred pounds, which was quite a lot of money, but then the blood in my body was worth a lot to me, too. I intended to protect it.

"Let me just polish that up for you," he said, "Get it nice and shiny."

As he took up the polishing cloth and began to buff my new vampire deflector, I asked him if he knew Sidney Lafontaine. I put her card down in front of him. He glanced up from the polishing and said, "You mean the estate agent? Yeah. Nice lady. She's got a client who'll pay top dollar for the string of shops on Harrington. My parents are all for it. They're ready to retire and the offer's generous. Your grandmother was planning to sell too. Well, makes sense really, all the shopkeepers on the street are older than dirt." He glanced up at me. "No offense."

Once again I had that disconnect between what Gran had stated in her will and the letter to me and what people who'd known her recently were saying. Where was the truth?

Before Peter rang up my purchase, I asked if they had any crucifixes for sale. He glanced at me curiously but he was too polite, or too British, to pry. Perhaps he thought I was Catholic, possibly even lapsed, and in my grief over my grandmother had decided to renew my faith. I let him think whatever he wanted, and walked out the owner of a sturdy wooden crucifix about six inches tall made of dark wood. Peter had suggested it was Spanish or Portuguese. I didn't care where it had come from so long as it did the job.

Back in the flat, I put together my anti-vamp kit in one of Gran's baskets—garlic, a jar of holy water, the crucifix and the sharpened wooden knitting needles. It looked like the strangest picnic ever.

The silver cross I planned to wear every day. It would make me feel more secure. If there were vampires in the knitting shop, they could be anywhere in Oxford.

EIGHT

DR. WEAVER'S SURGERY WAS located in a Victorian house near the old cholera graveyard on Walton Street. I rang to be let in, and walked down a short corridor into the very back of the building. There was a door with a small brass plaque that said, simply, *Dr. Christopher Weaver, GP.*

Inside, were several reclining chairs in a circle, much more deluxe than one usually finds in a doctor's waiting room. It was currently empty. As the door shut behind me, a gentleman emerged from an adjoining room and he introduced himself as Dr. Weaver.

We seemed to be the only two in the waiting room. There was no receptionist and no patients that I could see. I'd already had a very unnerving day, so maybe I was overreacting, but I was conscious of an urge to turn and flee. However, I'd come here for answers to how my grandmother died and I was determined not to let a bad case of the heebie-jeebies stop me in my quest.

"I'm Lucy Swift," I said. "Agnes Bartlett was my grandmother. I believe you signed her death certificate."

"Ah, Lucy. I'm very sorry about your grandmother." He was a small man, shorter than my own five feet six inches, and very dapper. He had a white beard trimmed close to his face, a large nose with so many broken blood vessels I suspected he drank, and brown eyes so dark it was like one huge pupil. He wore a white lab coat and beneath it I glimpsed a colorful red and navy waistcoat. "Please, come into my office."

I glanced back at the door, but then I told myself I was being foolish. So he had no patients at this second and no staff. That didn't make him sinister.

His office was ultramodern. A top-of-the-line computer was the only thing sitting on a white desk. Two leather chairs, also white, sat in front of the desk, and he settled himself behind it as he indicated I should have a seat in one of the visitors' chairs.

I said, "I understand you were the doctor who treated my grandmother at the end." He'd signed her death certificate, but somehow, having just seen my grandmother and spoken to her, the word death seemed inappropriate.

He nodded and touched a button on his computer. "I can either email you a copy of the MCCD, the Medical Certificate of Cause of Death, or print you out a copy if you'd like."

"Thank you. I'd like a printed copy. I do have a few questions, though."

"Of course."

"When I last saw my grandmother, about six months ago, she was perfectly healthy. And, every time we've emailed or phoned each other, she's been fine. So, I was very surprised to arrive in Oxford and discover that she was gone."

He nodded, gravely, his eyes soft and his voice gentle as he replied. "Even when we're prepared for these things, losing a loved one is a terrible shock. The truth is, your grandmother wasn't well, and hadn't been for some time. Congestive heart failure. I had seen her only a week before she died and at that time I encouraged her to be frank with her family about her condition. I didn't think she would go so soon, but I warned her she didn't have long. She was very much looking forward to your visit. I'm truly sorry she missed seeing you before she passed away."

Was he telling the truth? How would I know? "Congestive heart failure," I repeated. "You're certain that's what she died of."

"Of course," he said, but he looked down at his clasped hands as he said it.

"Did you see any signs of struggle, or an animal attack on my grandmother?"

He looked at me strangely. "An animal attack? In Oxford?"

"I thought perhaps a dog had bitten her."

He was looking at me as though I needed urgent medical treatment, so I said, "My grandmother was frightened of dogs. She'd been bitten as a young girl. I wondered if she'd had a run-in with a dog. That would have terrified her."

"I see. Yes. A shock like that could have

precipitated her final heart attack. But no. I'm not aware of any attack." He leaned forward, his elbows on the desk, "Your grandmother lived a good, long life, ran a successful small business, and was very proud of her family. She had great friends and was a pillar of our community. She died, as we'd all like to, peacefully in her sleep."

Had she, though? Then why was she wandering around her shop with bite marks on her neck? "I wish I'd been here." I so very much wished I'd come straight to Oxford instead of visiting my parents first.

He nodded. "Of course you do. But we all have to go sometime, my dear, and the truth is there's never a convenient time."

He pushed a button on the computer and a copy of the MCCD emerged from his printer.

He collected the printout and handed it to me. He didn't sit down again, a clear invitation to me to remove myself from his office. I rose, but said, "I do have another question. Who was the next of kin?" I'd done a bit of Google research and discovered that in the UK the MCCD is given to the next of kin who then take the form to the registry office to register the death. Without that step, my grandmother couldn't have been buried. My mother and I had both been unreachable.

Who, then, had made the funeral arrangements?

"Let me consult my notes." He went back around his desk and typed rapidly on his keyboard. "Ah, yes. As both you and your mother were out of the country and couldn't be reached, Agnes's niece, I suppose she'd be your cousin, took care of the details."

Agnes's niece? As far as I knew, Agnes didn't have a sister, so how could she have a niece? "Do you have her contact details?" I asked. Who was this supposed cousin? "I'd like to get in touch with her."

He looked surprised, as though I ought to know how to reach my own cousin. "Yes, I've got her address here somewhere." This time, he didn't touch the computer, but opened one of the drawers in the desk and retrieved a notebook. He flicked back a few pages and said, "Violet Weeks. Here we are. I'll write down the details for you, shall I?"

"Yes, please."

He wrote in a small, neat hand onto a prescription pad, then passed me the paper. "Thanks," I said. Violet Weeks lived in a place called Moreton-Under-Wychwood. On most days I'd have been charmed by the name of the village, but at that moment I simply felt numb.

The further I looked into my grandmother's death, the stranger it began to appear. Not only was my dead grandmother appearing out of the woodwork, but relatives I'd never known about seemed to be doing the same. I took the paper and prepared to leave. Then I turned, and asked him my final question. "Was my grandmother cremated or was she buried?"

He seemed to ponder the question. "Buried, I think."

"Do you have any idea where?"

"I'm sorry. I can't help you any more. Your cousin

will have that information."

"I hope someone does. I can't find anything online. No obituary was published in the local paper, there's no record of her funeral. I find that very strange."

"I believe it was a very small, private service, with only a few mourners in attendance. Perhaps because you and your mother were unavailable, your cousin felt it would be inappropriate to publish details about your grandmother's passing."

Perhaps, but it still smelled fishy to me—as did this whole situation.

I thanked him and as I left, a group of three college-aged kids entered holding printed forms. They saw me and said, "We're here about the notice." One waved it in front of me. "For the blood bank?"

"I don't work here," I said, and from behind me, Dr. Weaver said, "Yes, this is the place. Come in and have a seat." As they settled themselves on the comfortable loungers, he said, "And who already knows their blood type?"

* * *

I left with more questions than when I'd arrived. If my grandmother had suffered from congestive heart failure, why had she never told anyone? And how did I have cousins I'd never heard of?

More to the point, if my grandmother had died of congestive heart failure, as the doctor had written on this form in my hand, then what was she doing wandering around the knitting shop in the middle of the day? And what was all this about vampires? I knew one thing, at ten o'clock that night, I was going to be down in that shop.

* * *

Cardinal Woolsey's is usually welcoming. It's a tiny little corner of the world that's as timeless as knitting itself. The atmosphere is normally cheerful, cozy, and inviting. However, at a few minutes before ten that night, as I crept down the stairs wondering what I would do if I found the shop full of ghouls, Cardinal Woolsey's was none of those things. Frankly, I was terrified.

Nyx had watched me with green-gold eyes unblinking and her black tail twitching, as I made my preparations. I didn't want to come across as aggressive and confrontational if I was about to meet a nest of vampires, so I tucked the silver necklace into my T-shirt neck and slipped a cardigan over top so the large silver cross wouldn't show. That was the easy item to disguise.

The crucifix, garlic, and holy water were a little more tricky. I tried putting the crucifix in one pocket and the garlic in the other but it made the cardigan very lumpy. Also, it weighed down the two sides so it was clear that I had heavy things in each pocket.

I ended up loading the items in my handbag, hoping that if I needed to I'd be able to reach them quickly.

Mostly, I hoped I wouldn't need them at all. I'd get down there and find the shop dark and quiet and realize I had suffered some sort of hallucination.

The only thing I carried in my hands was a ball of bright pink knitting wool through which I had stuck the sharpened wooden knitting needles. Unless you looked carefully, they appeared harmless. It seemed reasonable that a person who had just inherited a knitting shop might wander around at night carrying a ball of wool and knitting needles.

As much as I wanted Nyx to come with me for the company, I had no idea whether vampires ate kittens. Did they? You never saw that in horror movies. I decided to leave her behind, but Nyx had a mind of her own and followed me. I took her back up and shut her into the flat, but she howled piteously.

With an irritated sigh, I returned again. This time, I put her out the window and shut it on her. She glared at me through the glass and then, turning her back pointedly, stalked along the ledge and jumped to the nearby tree.

Once more, I made my way downstairs to the shop. "Well," I said aloud, as I reached the door, "here we go."

I pushed open the door and walked into the knitting shop. Everything was quiet and still. I could barely make out the shapes of the baskets sitting quietly on the shelves. There was no noise, no sign of vampires; just the faintest smell of sheep's wool and the light fragrance I would always associate with my grandmother. I checked my cell phone for the time. Yes, I brought my cell phone, thinking I could always call the police if I had to.

I heard tapping at the shop door and, with my heart pounding and one hand in my handbag, opened it a crack. In ran Nyx.

After letting out a squeak of relief, that it wasn't a bloodthirsty vampire, I picked up the cat. She clearly wanted to be with me and her small, warm, body was a comfort. I decided to let her stay.

There was no one in the store, anyway. However, I couldn't turn around and run back to bed until I had checked the back room where Gran ran her classes. I headed toward the dark curtain that led into the back and paused feeling a chill run up my arm. Nyx's ears twitched.

There was no point standing out here, I had to know. I pulled the black curtain aside and the sight that met my eye was so extraordinary I almost fainted.

There were about a dozen knitters busily, and quietly, at work. The first thing I noticed? They didn't have pointed, bloodstained fangs, or black hair greased back in a widow's peak. They looked like normal people, though admittedly they were all rather pale. They sat in a circle and every single one of them, but one, was knitting.

My grandmother sat in the middle of them, her expression intent, fingers busy, needles taking a loop of wool from one needle to the next in a way that was so achingly familiar it made my heart hurt. The woman who looked like a movie star, Sylvia, sat beside her, knitting black leggings I think, or else a sweater for someone with extremely long arms. Rafe wasn't knitting, and he wasn't sitting down. He stood apart and I could tell he'd been watching for me.

He seemed almost angry to see me. "She's here." No greeting, no explanation. My grandmother glanced up and her beautiful smile lit up her face as it always did when she saw me. "Lucy. I'm so happy to see you again."

"I'm happy to see you, too." Though I have to admit I would have preferred her not to be dead.

Nyx struggled and, since none of the vampires seemed remotely interested in her, I put the cat down. She trod daintily forward on her skinny black legs straight up to my grandmother's chair then she dipped her haunches and in one smooth leap jumped onto my grandmother's lap. Gran glanced at the cat and then up at me. "Where did she come from?"

Of all the things I felt we had to talk about, a stray cat didn't seem the most important. "I don't know. She seems to be homeless. I'm keeping her until I can find her owner. Do you know who she belongs to?"

Gran was stroking the kitten under its chin and it bobbed its small head and purred loudly. "Oh yes. She's yours."

Had my grandmother got me a cat and died before she could tell me? If so, it was no wonder the poor thing was so skinny. It would mean she hadn't been fed in more than three weeks. Nyx didn't seem the kind who would meekly starve. She'd find another human willing to buy her lobster pâté and fancy tuna. "I'm not sure I understand."

She looked proud and excited. "Nyx is your familiar."

They all nodded as though they knew what she was talking about. "My familiar? Witches have familiars."

"Yes. And Nyx is yours."

If there was logic here, I wasn't grasping it. "I'm not a witch." And my grandmother wasn't a vampire. None of it made sense.

The vampires knitted on industriously but were clearly listening to every word. "It's time," Gran said.

"Time for what?"

"Your powers, dear. You're only beginning to feel them, aren't you?"

She chuckled, "You're a witch, from a long line of witches. Nyx here is your familiar. She'll help you."

She sounded as though this was good news, when I felt a creeping horror. "Wait, I'm twenty-seven-years old. Wouldn't I know by now if I was a witch?"

"You're a late bloomer. Always have been."

She was right. I was the last one in my class who could read. I couldn't tell time until I was eight. I still had trouble with left and right, and when all the other girls in high school were shopping at Victoria's Secret, I was still in a training bra. Now it seemed I was going to be the last student at Hogwarts to get my wand.

NINE

I WAS SO busy staring at Gran and trying to absorb the latest shock in a day full of them, that I didn't notice we had another knitter until Sylvia said, rather coquettishly, "Good evening, Doctor."

I turned and saw Dr. Weaver standing toward the back of the room. I had no idea how he'd come in because the door to the shop was locked, but I was beyond such simple questions anymore. He'd taken off the lab coat and now I saw that the colorful vest was hand-knitted in such tiny stitches it looked as though it would have taken years to create. He carried a green and blue knitting bag in his hands.

"Dr. Weaver!" I said, shocked.

He looked a bit sheepish. "Ah, Lucy. I wasn't sure how much you knew. I'm very sorry I misled you earlier, but we have to be very careful how much we tell the daywalkers."

"Come and sit here, Christopher," Sylvia said, gesturing to a wooden chair beside her own.

He nodded, but took the time to walk among the

knitters. "I think the silver thread on that cushion cover was inspired, Mabel," he said to a meek looking woman who looked as though she'd walked off the set of a WWII movie, complete with mousy brown hair in pin curls and a pale green twin set. Hand-knitted, of course. She'd have blushed if she'd still had the ability, I'm certain. "Thank you, Doctor," she said in a soft voice.

One of the vampires sneezed, an explosive sound in the quiet knitting circle. And then he sniffed, his long nose bobbing up and down like a bird's beak. "I smell garlic." He sneezed again. "I can't stand the stuff, I'm allergic."

"Don't be ridiculous, Alfred," Sylvia replied. "Do you think any of us are eating garlic anymore? I dream of garlic," she said dreamily, "sautéed in butter and white wine and served over scallops. With a steak, a nice, juicy steak."

A moan went up that seemed to come from all of them at once. "Stop!"

"It's me," I said feeling embarrassed. "I've got garlic in my bag."

The allergic vampire looked puzzled, as he drew out a neatly ironed cloth handkerchief and blew his nose. "Why would you bring garlic to a knitting meeting?"

Sylvia chuckled. "I suspect she thought it would protect her." She shook her head. "It's an old wives' tale." She glanced around at the circle. "The nonsense humans believe. The French vampires started that rumor about carrying garlic so their victims would arrive already seasoned."

"I'll go and put it in the other room," I said, feeling foolish.

Alfred, the allergic vampire, sneezed again and said thickly, "If you wouldn't mind."

I reasoned that if they wanted to attack me and suck all the blood out of my body they'd have done it by now. I didn't think six garlic bulbs would save me from a dozen hungry vampires. Anyway, they seemed more interested in their knitting than in the contents of my veins and arteries. Still, I left the crucifix and holy water in the bag, the silver chain around my neck, and I still carried the wool with the sharpened knitting needles.

My grandmother noticed the wooden needles when I returned from stashing the garlic in the other room and said, "Are you going to join us, dear? Have you been practicing your knitting?"

"No. I didn't come here to knit! I came to find out what's going on." It was ridiculous. I had just discovered that my grandmother was a vampire and here she was sitting in a knitting circle as though it was the most ordinary thing in the world, and the cat was curled up in her lap purring. I was surrounded by monsters from the darkest realm of history and mythology, and yet, standing here, I felt like the odd one out while they happily knitted on.

"Let me introduce you," Gran said, jumping suddenly into hostess mode. She glanced around. "Let's see, Rafe you know, of course, and Sylvia. She began to name each vampire and they would nod as I tried to remember the names.

One of them, an older, plump woman with apple cheeks and a sweet expression, called Clara, said, "I'll knit you a sweater, dear. What are your favorite colors?"

"No, wait. I want to knit her a sweater." This came from the goth girl with the petulant look on her face. Of course, she was a vampire. Her voice came out like a whine.

"Oh, grow up, Hester," Sylvia snapped.

The teenager glared at her. "I'm four-hundred-years-old."

Sylvia let out a long-suffering sigh. "Then try to act it."

The girl mimicked her, repeating her words, sounding more like ten than sixteen. Or four-hundred-and-sixteen. "And this is Hester," Gran said.

The sweet older woman, Clara, said, "We can all knit Lucy a sweater. It can get very cold here in the winter and it's always nice to have extras. Do you like blue?" Then she bent forward in her chair narrowing her gaze on my middle. "I don't suppose you're expecting? I do love to knit baby things. Those tiny booties are so sweet. And those little sweaters in pink and blue. I haven't done a layette in years."

"Seriously? You don't want to eat me, you want to knit me sweaters?" These were the most ridiculous vampires.

Once more, Rafe spoke. "Unlike mortals, we have a long time to work on a project. We've refined a way to get the blood we need without killing people."

"If it's got anything to do with the butcher's shop,

then I don't want to hear about it."

Sylvia wrinkled her nose. "Animal blood. Please." She glanced over at Dr. Weaver and then back at her knitting. "We have other sources."

"Wait a minute," I said, recalling the students sitting in those loungers at Dr. Weaver's surgery donating blood. I turned to the doctor, who was sitting beside Sylvia, working with needles as thin as Vermicelli, crafting himself yet another waistcoat. This one in black and red. "You're not running a blood bank at all. You're stealing blood from undergraduates."

"We don't steal it. We pay for it. And it's a small deception. They get extra pocket money and help keep the streets of Oxford safe." He smiled slightly. "A fed vampire is a happy vampire."

It still seemed wrong, and I was about to say so, when Rafe said, "We also have a connection at the hospital. The blood that's no good for transfusions, because it's stale or infected, doesn't end up in the incinerator. It comes to us."

"You drink tainted blood?"

He shrugged. "What's it going to do? Kill us?"

I supposed he had a point.

"The lovely, fresh, young blood Dr. Weaver provides is so much nicer, though," Alfred said. "Have you got the new supply with you? Is there lots of A positive? I'm very partial to A positive. I wish there weren't so many daywalkers with Type O. It doesn't agree with me. Gives me pains in the tummy."

Rafe still hadn't sat down, and if he had a knitting

project I saw no sign of it. "We're getting off-topic. Lucy wants to know why her grandmother is a vampire."

"Yep. That's about the size of it." Also there was the mysterious cousin, Violet Weeks, but I felt that of all the revelations from the last few hours, that one I could noodle out later. Preferably when I had Gran alone.

Sylvia sighed, put down her knitting, an exquisite shawl in blues and purples, and pushed her silver hair behind her ears. She really was the most elegant woman. "It's my fault. I turned your grandmother."

And this was the woman who'd wrinkled her nose at animal blood? I let the sarcastic notes seep into my tone, "And by turn, I assume you mean that you bit my grandmother on the neck and sucked all the blood out of her body?"

The woman's eyes grew deadly and she rose out of her chair with icy fury so fast that I wished I hadn't left the garlic in the other room. I was fumbling in my bag for the crucifix when Rafe put himself between us. "Sylvia! You forget yourself."

For a second she continued to glare at me and then she folded herself gracefully and resumed her seat. "I certainly didn't kill your grandmother. She's one of my dearest friends. It was the only way I could think of to save her."

Gran was watching her with affection so clearly she didn't harbor any resentment toward the woman who'd killed her.

I asked the obvious question. "Save her from what?" The most dangerous thing in the area had to be this nest of vampires. To my surprise, Sylvia reached for my grandmother's hand and spoke, not to me, but to her. "I'm sorry to put you through this again. I know it will be painful to listen to."

Gran nodded and I could see her fingers fold over as she squeezed the other woman's hand. "It's all right. Lucy needs to understand."

Sylvia paused before speaking and I felt that she was marshaling her thoughts. Again, I was reminded of an actress. There was the dramatic pause, as she made sure she had everyone's attention. Apart from the quiet, rhythmic clicking of knitting needles there was no sound. The stage was hers. "It was only by chance I was there. I woke early and thought I'd finish the border of the dress I'd been working on. I'd run out of the blue handspun wool I needed and so I came upstairs."

She paused, pressing her lips together as though the memory were painful. "It was about eight in the evening, I suppose, so the shop was closed.."

"Upstairs?" I was interrupting but I couldn't get my head around this idea that she lived downstairs. "There's nothing under here."

Rafe spoke again, somewhat dryly. "As I believe I mentioned, we've had plenty of time to work on our projects, such as our home. There are subterranean living quarters underneath the shop."

Did they call it a nest? I pictured rows of coffins tucked away but I was too eager to get back to the story to pry any more.

Since I seemed satisfied with his answer, Sylvia continued her story. "I paused on this side of the curtain, as I always do, to make sure the shop was empty. I heard a crash, a cry of pain. I thought I heard Agnes's voice. I didn't think, I ran into the shop calling her name. Her attacker fled out of the shop. A human man."

"You saved my life," Gran said. I wasn't sure how she was doing that math but I kept my mouth shut.

"I only wish I could have." Sylvia looked at me now. "Your grandmother was on the floor, moaning. At first I thought she'd interrupted a burglar who'd panicked and struck her with his fists. The shop was in chaos, baskets of wool on the floor, cabinets knocked over. ,I went to Agnes's side to try and revive her and get her to a doctor. Then, I saw the blood." She paused again, and I wasn't certain whether it was for dramatic effect, or because the memory was so painful. "She'd been stabbed."

I couldn't believe what I was hearing. "Stabbed? You mean with a knife?"

"Yes. I knelt by her side and started grabbing balls of wool, anything I could find, but I couldn't staunch the bleeding. She was near death when I got there and she was going fast. She said, "Tell Lucy. Must tell Lucy." I could feel that her spirit was about to leave her body and I acted instinctively. I turned your grandmother into a vampire. It was the only way I could save her."

I put my hands to my temples, the pink wool hot

and squished in my hand. There was so much new information in my brain that I was afraid my head would burst open if I didn't hold it all together. "You're saying that you turned my grandmother into a vampire just before she died of stab wounds?"

"Yes. It was too late to save her life. All I could do was make her immortal, one of us."

"I don't want to be rude, but how do I know that's the truth? Maybe you were hungry." I stepped back, behind Rafe, as I waited for that icy fury to come at me. She definitely glared at me, her eyes like two points of burning ice, but this time she controlled herself. "Doctor?"

"It's true," Dr. Weaver said. "Sylvia called me and I examined the bod—your grandmother. She was stabbed. Nothing could have saved her."

"But, if that's true, then you're saying that my sweet, beloved, grandmother, who runs a knitting shop, was, was—"

Rafe spoke the word I couldn't manage to say. " Murdered. Your grandmother was murdered."

TEN

I FELT AS though all the air had left my body, like an elephant had stepped on my chest and flattened my lungs. I've never fainted in my life but I think I was about to when suddenly Rafe was there putting his arm around me and leading me to one of the empty chairs. I sat and gently but firmly he pushed my head down between my knees and I sucked in air until the swirling black dots receded and my vision cleared.

I raised my head slowly. "I don't understand." I had said those words before. I felt I would say them many times yet to come. "Who would want to murder you, Gran?"

Gran shook her head, looking as confused as I felt. "I don't know. I simply don't know."

I rose and went to my grandmother's chair and squatted down in front of it. The cat eyed me, still purring. Gran looked troubled. "I wish you hadn't come. I don't want to think that you're in danger."

I laughed somewhat hysterically. "Apart from finding myself in the middle of a nest of vampires, why would I be in danger?"

"Don't be silly, dear, the members of the knitting club are our friends. But someone wanted to hurt me, and I can't get rid of the feeling that the danger may have passed to you."

"Why? Gran, who stabbed you?"

She shook her head. "I can't remember."

"All right," I said. "I want you to tell me everything you did that day."

She shook her head once more, regretfully. "That's the trouble. I can't remember that day at all."

Dr. Weaver pulled up a chair in front of mine. He wore the same expression he'd worn earlier when I went to see him in his office. I suppose it was his doctor-to-patient expression. "I believe the attack caused some kind of amnesia. The blow to the head, loss of blood, and the change, well, it's not surprising your grandmother's memory is impaired."

I put a hand to my forehead. "But you lied on an official government form and said that my grandmother died peacefully in bed. There's a murderer walking around free because of you."

Rafe spoke, cool and authoritative. "What would you have had him say? That your grandmother had been stabbed and then bitten in the neck by a vampire? We live peacefully here because we have a safe home and a ready supply of food, but make no mistake, if we ever find ourselves under attack, we will do what we must to protect ourselves." His words caused a chill to envelop me. I couldn't imagine the damage that a dozen, or two dozen or however many there were of them could do if they were hungry and enraged. They gave the term *hangry* new meaning.

I looked at Sylvia. "You said my grandmother's last words were about me?"

"Yes. She said, 'Tell Lucy. Must tell Lucy.'"

I was pleased to hear that she had repeated the words the second time exactly the same way I had heard them the first, which suggested that that was, in fact, what she had heard my grandmother say. I turned to Gran, "What do you think you meant?"

"Oh, how I wish I knew. I've racked my brain to try and remember something, anything."

Once more I spoke to Sylvia. "And the person you saw running out of the shop? The attacker. Can you describe them at all?"

"It all happened in such a blur. It was one person, I only saw their back briefly, I was more worried about your grandmother. I think they wore black boots."

In a college town like Oxford, that was going to narrow it down. "Male or female?" I asked.

"I assumed male but now, now I don't know."

"Were they tall? Or short? Fat or thin?"

She closed her eyes and I could see that the effort she was making to come up with something. "The boots were shiny. I think they were new."

Dr. Weaver said. "You'd be surprised how many of the freshers come to school wearing new shoes."

"You think a student did this?"

He shrugged. He didn't know. None of them did.

And a murderer had gone free.

I studied the circle of knitting vampires. Apart from being rather pale, they could have been any knitting circle anywhere. No, I thought, as I looked more carefully, they were knitting with astonishing speed. One woman's fingers moved so quickly they blurred my vision. She wore her hair piled on top of her head and a drab looking dress with long sleeves and a high neck. Its skirt went to the floor. On her feet were leather button-up boots. She sat so straight in her chair that she might have been wearing a corset. Or perhaps she was. She was chattering away to the woman beside her in a low voice, but I heard snatches of conversation. "The doctor was ever so good. He thinks it's my rheumatism acting up."

I turned to Rafe who was standing at my side. "Rheumatism?"

"That's Silence Buggins."

I raised my eyebrows. "Silence?"

"It was one of the virtue names common in Victorian times. Not a virtue this woman is noted for, however."

Silence, in fact, seemed to be a chatterbox. Also a hypochondriac. She'd now moved on to some vague stomach complaint. I wasn't very up on vampire lore and, anyway, as in the garlic myth, some of it had to be wrong, but did they really have all the aches and pains of humans?

"Rheumatism?"

He glanced at me. "She likes the attention. Dr.

Weaver sees her regularly and always gives her a tonic that makes her feel better." He leaned in, "Placebo effect." I imagined I knew what was in the tonic.

Clara, the sweet older vampire said, "Well, this has been a most eventful evening. I barely managed two rows." She folded her work and put it into a large tapestry knitting bag. "If you don't mind, dear, I'll pop out front and choose some wool. I've got an idea in mind for that sweater for you, with your fair hair and pretty blue eyes."

I had no idea how this worked. Did Gran let the vampires help themselves from her stock? That wasn't much of a way to run a business.

As though she had read my mind, Clara smiled at me. "We have a very simple system. We keep track of what we take and once a month we pay up our accounts."

"How do you pay?" I had this image of being handed Doubloons or pieces of gold fished out of ancient leather bags. She said, "Direct debit is easiest. But lately I've been experimenting with Bitcoin."

I could see that all the vampires were gathering their knitting and putting their projects away. "Are you all leaving?"

Alfred, the sharp-nosed vampire who was allergic to garlic, said, "Normally at this stage of the meeting we do a show-and-tell and discuss our projects and what we're planning to work on next. But, we've gone over time as it is."

I looked at Rafe as though he could explain this

bizarre behavior. These knitters were undead and immortal, what were they in a hurry to get to? He said, "You have to remember that we're cooped up all day. There are only a few hours of complete darkness, and that's when we go out and take our exercise, or do our visiting."

"Visiting. Right." I envisioned the lady vampires sitting over a teapot discussing the merits of Type A and Type O as though they were Earl Grey and Darjeeling. No doubt they drank their favorite type out of china teacups.

Gran, as the newest vampire, looked a little unsure of what she was meant to do. I was about to ask her to come upstairs with me. I imagined that we could talk and catch up, but Sylvia took her arm and helped her to stand. She said, "Come on, Agnes. A good brisk walk will do you good. And then there's that new exhibit at the Ashmolean we've been wanting to see."

Gran turned to me. "Try and get some sleep now, love. I'll see you tomorrow."

I didn't want to let her go. "Promise?" I asked.

"Yes, of course."

Rafe said in a low voice, "It's important for her to develop routines and work out how she's going to get along in her new life. Sylvia will look after her."

I nodded, but it was hard for me to see my grandmother walk further back into the shop with the other members of the vampire knitting club. The man with a sharp nose shifted the old rug and lifted a trapdoor that I wouldn't have known was there and one by one they disappeared down below the shop. Rafe remained. He looked at me and said, "This has been a lot for you to take in."

And wasn't that the understatement of the millennium? Now that my grandmother had gone and taken her lap with her, Nyx returned to my side. Rafe said, "Why don't we go upstairs and I'll answer some of the questions you're no doubt dying to ask."

I'd rather it was my grandmother explaining things to me, but I got the feeling that she probably didn't know. She was a baby vampire. And Rafe was, what? I looked at him. "How old are you?"

He smiled briefly. "One day I'll tell you."

I didn't know that vampires were vain about their ages. But then I didn't know much about vampires at all.

He said, "In all the drama of hearing about your grandmother's death, I think there's one piece of information tonight that you may not have taken in."

I stood with my hands on my hips and looked at him. "You mean the part where my grandmother told me I'm a witch? No, I didn't miss that at all."

* * *

Rafe and I, accompanied by Nyx, went upstairs. There was no point standing in the knitting shop after hours, not with this new knowledge cloaking me like a curse. Yesterday I'd been far too careful to invite a sexy stranger up into my living space. Today, the world was a different place. My grandmother was a vampire and I, apparently, was a witch.

"What kind of witch gets to be twenty-seven years old and has no idea of her powers?" I felt like an abject failure. "Shouldn't there have been some kind of signs? Mysterious happenings? Like I might get angry and suddenly a tornado would appear? Or a boy would break my heart and suddenly be turned into a toad? Wait, there was this guy named Todd—"

"I doubt very much you've turned anyone into a toad, or started any tornadoes or bad weather patterns. Being a witch isn't like being a vampire. You don't one day get bitten and next thing you're wandering around immortal and undead. Witches are born special, but spells must be learned and practiced, and I believe turning a human into an amphibian is one of the more difficult of the spells."

I rolled my eyes, "Do you know everything?"

"I've had a lot of years to study, a lot of time to read. I know a great deal."

"Did you know I was a witch? When you first met me?"

He sat on my grandmother's couch, the one across from the window, even though it was full dark outside. I imagined it was force of habit. I sat across from him and Nyx jumped on my lap.

"When I saw that cat prowling outside your door, I had a pretty good idea."

"I don't know the first thing about being a witch. Will I grow warts on my nose and have to live in a stone cottage way out in the woods somewhere? Will children run in fear when they see me?"

"You've been reading too many fairytales. You will learn to heal, possibly to help people in trouble, and you may get ideas about the future."

"I could go to medical school for most of that."

"You could." He seemed to think the idea of me suddenly going into med school with no prerequisites a normal idea. I suspected that where he came from, and *when* he came from, becoming a doctor was a lot easier. Besides, I had no aptitude for science or any desire to take years of training.

"It's been quite a day. I think I need a drink." I went into the kitchen and dug through the cupboards. I brought out the Harvey's Bristol Cream, which seemed to be the only alcohol my grandmother kept in stock. I waved the blue glass bottle in his direction. "Would you like a glass of sherry?"

He grimaced. "I don't think I could choke down another glass."

"The way shocks keep coming my way, I'm going to have to invest in a bottle of brandy. Maybe a case." In the meantime, I poured a large glass of sherry and sat down across from Rafe. I was too much Agnes's granddaughter not to be upset that I was enjoying refreshment while my guest had nothing. "Can I get you anything?"

"I ate earlier," he said.

I didn't want to inquire too closely so I just nodded and took another sip of the sweet sherry. I repeated the thought that had been going around and around my head ever since Sylvia had told her story. "Who would want to harm my grandmother?"

He shook his head. "I wish I knew. I should have been here. I was in New York evaluating a private collection and preparing it for auction. If I'd been here, perhaps I'd have been able to stop the attack."

He looked so sad that I found myself reassuring him. "How could you have known? How could anyone have known that she'd be attacked in her own shop like that?"

"It's unthinkable."

"There must've been a reason. There wouldn't be enough in the till that robbery could be the motive. I'm certain she didn't have any enemies." I glanced at him under my lashes and decided to test the only theory I had. "Are we sure that Sylvia's telling the truth?"

He looked to me sharply. "What do you mean?"

"I don't know much about vampires but I'm going to take a guess that fresh blood that you suck out of a dying victim is sweeter than anything you're getting from a blood bank. I'm wondering whether Sylvia was overcome with hunger, and after she killed my grandmother made up that story to protect herself."

He shook his head. "The doctor did examine your grandmother's body. She had definitely been stabbed and there was a contusion on her head consistent with having hit it on the radiator when she fell."

"It makes no sense."

"Your grandmother's right about one thing. Since

we don't know why she was killed, how do we know that you're not in danger? There's nothing holding you here, Lucy. If you want to head back to America no one would be surprised. At least you'd be safe."

What kind of person did he think I was? I put the glass down so it clicked on the coffee table. "There is no way I'm going back home until I have some answers. Someone all but murdered my grandmother and I intend to find out who."

I'd been wondering whether I would stay and run the knitting shop or go back home and try and figure out what I wanted to do with my life. At least, now, I had an immediate goal. I was going to reopen Cardinal Woolsey's and I was going to keep my eyes and ears open, ask around the neighborhood, do whatever I could to find out who wanted my grandmother dead.

* * *

I woke the next morning filled with determination. No one attacked Gran and got away with it. Not on my watch. I found an old notebook with pictures of flowers on the front cover and opened it to a clean page. I decided to make yet another list.

What did I know? If I believed Sylvia and the other vampires, and I wasn't at all sure that I did, then Gran had been stabbed nearly to death. Sylvia, the vampire with a heart of gold, had turned her in order to save her. And Sylvia had seen someone in shiny black boots running away from the crime. It wasn't much to go on.

I wrote down the questions that sprang immediately to my mind. Obvious ones first.

One: Who would want to kill my grandmother and why?

Actually, that was really the main question that I had. All the other ones led to its answer.

I tapped my pen against the page and began to think. Sylvia didn't remember much, but if her timing was right, and it had been about eight o'clock in the evening when she had interrupted the attack on my grandmother, then the shop would have been closed, and the door locked. In spite of the fact that vampires seemed to come and go with complete disregard for locked doors, most people were less agile. I was going to assume that the murderer was human —otherwise, why would there be stab wounds?

The dense fog of confusion that had surrounded me since I had discovered at one and the same time that my grandmother was a vampire and that she believed I was a witch began to dissipate now that I had something concrete to do.

I put the whole witch thing aside. Surely, if I were a witch, there would have been some clues in the last twenty-seven years. The only odd thing about me was that I came late to things. That and the vivid dreams. But lots of people had vivid dreams and didn't turn out to be witches.

Perhaps I could test myself. I looked on the Internet but all the spells I found seemed to involve burying things in the back garden, saying some rhyming words and poof, in a month or so your hair would be thicker, that skin condition might have cleared up, or that guy you'd been crushing on might notice you. Of course, I reasoned, people who posted spells online probably weren't real witches, and all of those things could be coincidence. I wanted something I could do now and see results.

I glanced around and focused on the botanical prints Gran had hung in the dining room. There was an apple, a pomegranate, and a leek. The prints were old and hand-colored. I'd always thought three fruits in a row would be better than two fruits and a vegetable. Seemed a harmless way to test my powers. I came up with a simple rhyme, something like what I'd seen online.

In that frame there shouldn't be a leek
A blushing pear is what I seek
As I decree
So let it be

I walked into the dining room and said the words, staring at the leek as I did, with its bulbous bottom and trailing root. Not that I'd expected a flash of fire and presto, the picture would change, but I admit I was a bit let down when nothing at all happened.

Not that my hopes had been high, but it seemed I wasn't a witch after all.

I could move on.

I walked back to the living room and resumed my seat. After retrieving my notebook, I settled back to think, but couldn't get comfortable. Something was digging into my back. I shifted the cushions and finally stood and pulled the faded chintz cushion off the couch. Behind it was a roll of paper, quite old, and a bit frayed at the edges. I unrolled it and there was a botanical print of a single pear, hanging from a bit of branch, with a few leaves above it. There were a couple of brown spots, exactly like a real pear's skin, and where the sun had shone on it, the artist had colored it a reddish, terra cotta color. *A blushing pear is what I seek.*

But if I'd magically caused the pear print to appear, why hadn't it appeared in front of me as I'd intended? No doubt Gran had bought this print intending to have it framed to add to her collection and this was one of those very coincidences that make gullible people believe in magic.

I laid the rolled print on the dining table. I'd ask Gran if she'd purchased it, though, with her bad memory lately there was no guarantee she'd remember.

Back to the late night visit. Either the perpetrator of this crime had a key to the door, or my grandmother had felt comfortable enough to open the door to them long after the shop was closed. I added another question to my list. Who had keys to the shop door?

Then I added another item to my to do list. *Change locks*. I'd intended to do it yesterday, but with all the drama hadn't got around to it.

There is a wonderful saying about not putting off until tomorrow what you can do today. And, something about a possible murderer having a key to the shop downstairs was enough to get me pulling out my mobile. I fetched my laptop and did a search of locksmiths in the area. I made four phone calls before I could find a locksmith who could come that very day. We made an arrangement for two that afternoon and I felt marginally better. I had something on my to do list that I could cross out.

I couldn't stop the picture forming in my head of my beloved grandmother fighting for her life and some evil person taking it from her. I was determined, as I had never been determined before, to get justice for Gran. I felt suddenly like Scarlet O'Hara standing in the ruins of Tara with her fist raised in the air crying, "As God is my witness, I'll never go hungry again."

Well, as God was my witness, I would avenge Gran's murder.

As the surge of righteous anger filled me, I became aware of another sensation, like electric impulses going up my arm and through my fingertips. I looked down and gasped. Flashes of white and blue light danced across the ends of my fingertips. There was no way I could blame this light show on static electricity.

"No," I whispered. It couldn't be possible, could it? Was Gran right and I'd just found out, at the ripe old age of twenty-seven years old, that I was a witch.

I took a deep breath and rubbed my hands together and that stopped the light, but not the thoughts racing through my head. Okay, I had to focus. Being a witch was crazy and terrifying and life altering, but right now I had to solve my grandmother's murder. I couldn't afford to be bewitched by my own abilities.

I looked at my hands, now perfectly ordinary hands,

with fingers that could use a manicure but otherwise appeared unremarkable. What if that light-zapping thing happened when I was out somewhere in public? I pictured myself reaching out to accept a block of cheese from the cheese mongers and suddenly blue and white light jumping out of my fingertips. There'd been more than a few witches burned at the stake in Oxford. Even if they didn't roast my kind anymore, like marshmallows over a campfire, I did not relish the thought of anyone knowing about this strange and very unwelcome quirk.

Why couldn't my newfound powers tell me whether the murderer had been known to my grandmother? That would be a lot more helpful than firestarters for fingers and pear prints that arrived unframed. Gran was so kindhearted, could she have opened the door to someone pretending to be in need? Was a serial killer on the loose?

Instead of adding that question to the list, I went online. There was no news story about an out-of-control knife-wielding murderer on the prowl. That didn't mean there wasn't one. However, I've always heard that the vast majority of murders are committed by people known to the victim. I thought I'd start there.

But who would kill the proprietor of a knitting shop? I knew all about the frustration of wool that insisted on tangling up in itself instead of knitting properly, and patterns clearly devised by the minions of hell to confuse a person. I may have once or twice stabbed a ball of wool, quite savagely, with a pair of knitting needles, but killing the knitting shop owner seemed a little extreme. Still, I'd keep my eyes on the customers and see if there was anyone who seemed dangerous.

Could there be enemies from her past that I didn't know anything about? I realized how little I actually knew about my grandmother. I would have to learn what I could about her background and see if that's where the mystery lay.

And then there was Violet Weeks, my supposed cousin and Gran's niece. I wondered if that were true, or a fib devised by Dr. Weaver and his vampire chums to get my gran quietly buried, and fast. I should have demanded more answers of Dr. Weaver. I was not a very good sleuth.

At least I'd decided to open the knitting shop the next day. It would give me something to do other than brood, and I would get to know some of her patrons.

The living ones.

ELEVEN

I HAD NO idea whether I'd have any customers in Cardinal Woolsey's on Friday when we reopened. Still, I had to make a start. I'd spent yesterday updating the website and the shop's social media pages and having the locks changed.

I messaged Rafe, reminding him about the reopening, and asked him to pass the information on to the rest of the undead knitters, with a special request that someone keep an eye on Gran so she didn't inadvertently wander into the shop halfway through the day.

Until she became more used to her new role as a creature of the night, her insomnia could be a real problem. He promised that they'd post shifts to keep an eye on Gran and wished me luck on my first day.

I put on a plain black skirt over leggings and short boots that I thought might be reasonably comfortable for standing most of the day. On top I wore a simple white T-shirt and added the silver chain and cross by way of jewelry. Of course I believed the vampires living beneath me got their meals from a blood bank, but until they became accustomed to a warm-blooded person upstairs, I thought I'd play it safe.

I'd put the vampire repelling items into a basket that was tucked away in a corner of the back room.

My hair is long and naturally curly, which is much more annoying than people with straight hair have any idea of, and it wasn't behaving. I looked at my fingers. Should I attempt a good hair spell? Then I thought of the electricity that seemed to burst out of my fingertips randomly and pictured myself with hair sticking straight out in all directions, like Nyx when she had a fright. I left my hair loose and, what some people might call messy, and I prefer to call quirky. I put on a little mascara and some lip gloss and called it a day.

I was about to head down to the shop when Nyx meowed piteously. I'd thought she was out, but it seemed she was stuck somewhere. Sure enough, I found her shut inside Gran's bedroom. She must have gone in and then the door closed behind her. "What are you doing in here?" I asked her. She gave me a look that basically said, "When are you going to realize I don't talk?"

"I'm lonely and nervous. Give me a break."

I swear she shook her head at me. She was sitting on top of Gran's wooden jewelry box. It had been a treasure box to me when I was a kid. The lid lifted up and all the coiled costume jewelry necklaces and sparkly earrings had seemed like pirate's booty. Nyx jumped down as I approached and walked out the door.

I was about to follow her, but then I looked at the jewelry box and thought how much I'd like to wear something today that was Gran's, for good luck. When I raised the lid, a scent emerged that reminded me of all the times Gran and I had played dress-up. Her ruby ring was sitting in a velvet lined tray. The ring was quite plain. A round, dark red stone set in gold filigree. She'd always worn it. I slipped it on my own finger and found it fit perfectly and was comforting. I'd carry a part of her with me into her shop.

Somehow, wearing that ring, I felt more prepared as I headed downstairs, Nyx at my side.

I opened the door leading into the shop and as I entered my foot bumped into a cloth shopping bag. I knew it hadn't been there last night when I'd locked up behind the locksmith.

Curious, I picked up the bag. When I'd turned all the lights on, I looked inside to find a blue hand-knit cardigan with an exquisite pattern of flowers and butterflies knitted into the front. As I took the sweater out of the bag I saw the note. It read, "Good luck on your first day. Love from all of us in the knitting club."

It was only two days ago that Clara had offered to knit me a sweater and now it was done. As I slipped my arms into the sleeves I began to think my first day running Cardinal Woolsey's was getting off to a good start.

Nyx walked around the perimeter poking her nose into baskets and sniffing corners, presumably on the hunt for mice. I was heartily glad she didn't find any and, instead, wandered to the window display, jumped up and stepped into the basket of assorted wools I'd arranged yesterday. She turned her body around a few times, pawed at the balls of wool until she was satisfied and then curled herself up and closed her eyes.

I couldn't decide whether to toss her out or let her sleep, when I heard the door rattle. It was a couple of minutes before nine. I opened the door and Rosemary stood there looking as though it was a great imposition to have to come to work. She'd always dressed for comfort rather than style and today was no different. She wore a flowered smock over a pair of brown stretch pants and white trainers. She was probably around sixty, with permed red hair and high color in her cheeks, as though she suffered from elevated blood pressure.

Deciding to start out on a good footing with my one and only employee, I gave her a warm smile and wished her a good morning.

She blinked and mumbled, "Morning."

"You're probably wondering why your key wouldn't work, but I had the locks changed yesterday. Not knowing how many people might have Gran's key made me nervous."

Rosemary hefted her bulk into the shop and her mouth turned down. "She made me give my key back."

"I beg your pardon?" Surely, I hadn't heard her correctly.

"My key. After the break-in, your grandmother suddenly got worried and asked for my key back. As if Randolph would have anything to do with it." She looked at me belligerently, as though I might argue with her.

I was completely confused. This was the first I'd heard of a break-in. "Randolph? Who's Randolph?"

Her glare intensified. "He's my son, and he's a good boy. Ever since he came out of the nick, he's been as good as gold."

"Your son was in prison?" No wonder Gran had taken back her key. I didn't want to ask the next question but I knew I had to. "What was he in for?"

"Just a bit of petty thieving. But since he came out he's been ever so good. He's kept that job down at the charity shop, and he sees his parole officer regular like."

"I see." I'd planned to give Rosemary one of the new sets of keys, but now I decided to hold onto them. I'd let my assistant in myself in the morning and make sure I locked up at night after she'd left. "When was the break-in?"

"I told you my Randy had nothing to do with it." I thought she might hit me with the large canvas bag she held gripped in her hands.

"I'm sure he didn't, but I don't know anything about this break-in. When did it happen? Was anything taken?"

She seemed slightly mollified that I hadn't accused her son and relaxed her grip on the bag. "Couple of months ago, it was. The lock had been forced."

"Did Gran report it to the police?" I was surprised Ian Chisholm hadn't mentioned it.

Rosemary shook her head. "Nothing was taken, see?

Your gran didn't see the point in reporting a broken door, 'cause that's all it was." She glanced around the shop and not with affection. "Well, stands to reason. Who'd break down a door to take a bunch of wool? There's not enough left in the till at night to bother with."

"Had they tried to open the till?"

"Don't think so. Your gran reckoned they was drunk or heard somebody coming and ran off." She put her bag in the cupboard under the cash register and sighed. "I was so sorry about your poor old grandma." Something about the way she said the words set my teeth on edge. She sounded smarmy and insincere. My hand felt hot suddenly and when I glanced down I saw that Gran's ruby ring was glowing, so slightly only I could see it, but it was glowing all the same. Between fingers that sparked electric storms and a ring that glowed all on its own I was beginning to feel like a freak.

I didn't like Rosemary and I didn't like the sound of the thieving son at all. I'd have to ask Gran if she knew anything about him.

When I didn't respond to her false sympathy, she immediately gushed over my new sweater. She identified every bit of wool that had been used in the sweater, all of which we carried. "But wherever did you get it? I'm sure you don't know how to knit like that."

"Nope. I'm still the world's worst knitter." I couldn't tell her the truth, obviously, so I said I had found the sweater upstairs and thought I'd wear it to remind me of my grandmother. "If anyone wants to make one, we can gather together the supplies. Do you think this knitting pattern's from the shop?"

She put her head to one side and studied me. "No. I'd say that's done freehand. But I can find something in our pattern books that would be similar."

"Excellent. I just hope we have some customers today."

I need not have worried that there'd be no business on our first day open. I'd barely flipped over the open sign when three young women walked in. Two had backpacks over their shoulders and one carried a book bag. One wore a sweatshirt with the name of her college embroidered on it. They were in their early twenties, and looked confident, intelligent, and very much at ease in my grandmother's shop. One of the three stepped forward as I came around from behind the cash desk to greet them. She said, "We're so happy you're open today. We were awfully sorry to hear about the lady who used to run it. She was so nice, and always ready to help if you got in a muddle with a pattern."

"Yes, she was. She was my grandmother. I'm Lucy."

The confident girl who seemed to be their spokesperson said, "We're all reading law and some of those lectures would do your head in if you didn't have knitting to keep you busy. I'm making scarves for all my friends at Christmas, and now my dad says he wants a sweater."

I loved the mental image of the three of them sitting in their lectures knitting away, and was pleased to hear them speak so highly of my grandmother. "You probably know better than I do where everything is. Let us know if we can help you."

All three purchased wool and patterns. While we were ringing up their purchases the talkative one asked, "Are you going to offer knitting classes again? They were so good."

I didn't even know if I was going to keep the shop open, never mind schedule knitting classes. "I'll put our schedule up on the website as soon as it's finalized."

As I was ushering them out of the store, two older women came in and raved about my new sweater. Rosemary collected the various wools and showed them the pattern she had found that came closest to what I was wearing. The elder of the two said, "That would look lovely on my granddaughter. I'll take the wools and the pattern."

I silently thanked Clara, my sweet vampire knitter.

A woman came in soon after, glanced around, and asked, "Do you do brioche?"

"Brioche? The French bread?" I remembered Gran's adage that every customer deserved to be treated with respect, even if they came into a knitting store looking for baked goods. "You might try the tea shop, next door."

My customer looked around, confused. Rosemary overheard me and laughed, a very superior, nasal sound. "Lucy, she means *Brioche Knitting*. It's a very popular knitting technique." She took over from me, which was fine, but I could have done without her condescending explanation. "Lucy's new here. She doesn't know much about knitting."

She knows about paying your salary, though.
Traffic in the shop stayed steady after that. A few times we even had a lineup for the till. I was glad I had an assistant who knew where most things were and could answer complicated questions about knitting. She had noticed right away that the wools were horribly out of order and whenever there was a lull went to work putting things back the way my grandmother had always kept them.

I let her go for lunch at noon and so I was alone when a man walked in shortly after she'd left. He was the kind of person who seemed to bring a burst of energy with him. Somewhere in his forties and outrageously handsome, with a tan that suggested he spent winters in Spain, dazzling white teeth, and dark eyes, he looked around the shop with a sense of delight. "I never walk into this charming shop without feeling I'm stepping into the past. It's a perfect little slice of history. All the shops along this road are like that."

Did he knit? He didn't look like a knitter but then, as I had discovered, there really was no stereotypical knitter. At least not in Oxford. "I've always loved this street. Can I help you with something?"

"I was so happy to see the store open today and be able to come and give you my condolences in person. What terrible news on the loss of dear Agnes."

So many people today had given me their condolences and each time I felt a stab of pain in the region of my heart as I was reminded once more that Gran, at least the mortal woman who had been my grandmother, was gone. I nodded. "Thank you."

"And you must be her beautiful granddaughter? I've heard so much about you from your grandmother."

"Really? That's nice."

He laughed, showing more of those dazzling teeth. I was certain he'd whitened them. "You're wondering if I knit. I must admit, every time I come into the shop I'm tempted to take up the hobby. Heaven knows, my wife would be only too pleased if I would sit still for five minutes. But I have too much energy. No, I've been speaking to your grandmother on a business matter." He glanced behind him but we were alone. "I think my estate agent has been in. Ms. Lafontaine? Sidney Lafontaine?"

I nodded, not looking encouraging. He was clearly a man who didn't waste time on silence. "I know your grandmother wanted to discuss the proposal with you. That's why I know so much about you. She respected you enormously, and said you had training in business."

Well, two years of business college because I couldn't decide what I wanted to be when I grew up.

He looked at me expectantly. "Did she?"

"Did she what?"

"Discuss my proposal? I'm Richard Hatfield," he said as though I would immediately know the name. "No doubt your grandmother spoke of me."

I shook my head. "I hadn't heard anything until Sidney Lafontaine came in. Perhaps Gran was waiting until I arrived."

"Well, she was very excited about my proposal. Very excited." He took a deep breath in a rather dramatic fashion. "I hate to be indelicate, but do you know who inherits? When your grandmother passed away, she hadn't signed the contract, but she intended to. Now that she's gone, I think my plan makes excellent sense for the new owner of Cardinal Woolsey's and this property. I believe she has a daughter, that would be your mother. Is she the sole beneficiary?"

I hesitated to inform the somewhat pushy man that I was the one he should be speaking to so, instead, I said, "Why don't you explain your proposal to me? As you said, my grandmother liked to talk over business matters with me. My mother's difficult to get hold of right now."

He looked as though pitching me would be the greatest pleasure on earth. "Excellent idea."

The bell jingled indicating that I had new customers and, when I looked behind Richard Hatfield, I saw a middle-aged couple entering. "For heaven's sake don't be in here all day," the man grumbled, in a hopeless way as though he knew perfectly well she wouldn't listen to him.

His wife said, "Go and walk up and down the street if you want to. Or go next door and have a cup of coffee. I'll come and find you when I'm finished."

He gave a jeering laugh. "No thanks. I'll stay here and make sure you don't spend too much money." He saw that Richard Hatfield and I were both looking at him and spoke to Richard, man-to-man, "You know what they're like. How they can spend so much on something that they have to make themselves is beyond me. You could buy a sweater at Marks & Spencer for half the price of what she spends on her wool and her knitting needles and her buttons and I don't know what."

The woman looked at her husband as though she would happily take a couple of knitting needles off the wall and poke him with them. She said sweetly, "Imagine how many sweaters I could knit for the price of your golf membership."

He mumbled something under his breath and headed to the single chair we kept for visitors. I had the sense that this argument played and replayed itself.

Richard Hatfield turned back to me. "It's a rather time sensitive issue. Why don't I come at the end of the day? Perhaps I could take you for a drink and we could talk? Or, we could have lunch? If you haven't eaten yet?"

I thought lunch would be much easier than a drink after work. And if he was telling the truth, and Gran had been interested, I should hear him out. "I could meet you next door at Elderflower at one o'clock."

He glanced at his watch. It was big and round and seemed to have a variety of functions. This was the watch of a man to whom time was precious. "Roughly half an hour from now. Yes, that's perfect. I'll see you there."

As I rang up the woman's purchases, her husband pulled himself to his feet and came over, scowling. When I announced the total he threw his hands in the air. "Good Lord. It's the national debt."

"Oh do shut up, Harry."

TWELVE

THE ELDERFLOWER TEA Shop was busy with the lunch crowd when I arrived, and I imagined I'd have to wait, but Richard Hatfield was already seated and he waved to me from a table he had managed to snag in the only quiet corner. He rose politely as I reached the table. "Excellent. You made it." He gave me his charming grin. "The specials are broccoli quiche with salad and chicken pie. The soup of the day is potato and leek. I'm having the quiche." I agreed that sounded good, and he waved a hand to summon the waitress. It wasn't one of the Miss Watts, but a young woman with a French accent. She took our order and then left.

He said, "I won't beat about the bush. I love this little corner of Oxford. I've been coming here since I was a boy."

"Really?" I was surprised. I don't understand British accents the way British people do. They can practically pinpoint where a person came from and how wealthy they are every time they open their mouths. But I knew enough to know that he didn't have the elegant, upper-class accent that I heard so often in Oxford.

He said, "I grew up in South London, but I had an auntie who lived here and we used to visit her in the summers. She'd take me to the little grocer's up the road, and buy me sweets.

"We'd go for tea in this very tea shop. She didn't knit, so we never went into your grandmother's knitting shop. She did like to poke around Pennyfarthing Antiques, though I think it was called something else then. I got a few lead soldiers there. I still have them."

Our food came then and as we settled to our meal, he said, "Coming here is quite literally a walk down memory lane. And, I don't want to appear rude, but as recent events have shown us, the proprietors of these shops are not young. I'm proposing to buy all four of the shops in this row."

"You want to buy Cardinal Woolsey's?" I wanted to be absolutely certain that I had understood what he was getting at.

He put down his knife and fork and gestured widely. "Not only Cardinal Woolsey's but this tea shop and the antique shop and the gift shop."

I'd heard that Oxford was second only to London in its property prices, so to buy up four shops he was talking about a lot of money.

"Why What's in it for you to buy a string of shops? These buildings are all listed, you know?"

He looked at me approvingly. "Americans are so direct. I like that. The simple truth is I am buying the properties for an investment. They'll continue to increase in value over the years and I will have the pleasure of knowing that these charming little shops I have loved since I was a boy will remain as they were."

I put down my knife and fork and drilled him with my gaze. I might be young, but I wasn't stupid. "Usually when developers buy a series of properties at once, they plan to knock them down and build something else."

"Not me. I simply want to preserve them."

I thought of my unorthodox roommates living beneath the shop and I knew I could never let the old building be torn down. Besides, there were all sorts of rules and regulations regarding heritage buildings. I was certain the facades had to be preserved but a little fuzzy on what was permitted inside. Still, he must have very deep pockets to plan to purchase most of a block. I narrowed my eyes. "You definitely won't knock them down?"

"Not unless they are structurally unsound."

"Well, they've been standing for hundreds of years. I imagine if they were structurally unsound, they'd have fallen down by now."

"Exactly."

As the new owner of Cardinal Woolsey's and the building, I was being offered my freedom on a silver platter. However, I knew the contents of my grandmother's will, and now I knew why she had stipulated that the knitting shop must remain in my care.

"And you would preserve them? Exactly as they are?"

"That's what I'm saying."

It was almost too good to be true. What if I could give my grandmother what she had wanted, and still be able to do whatever I wanted? Of course, I didn't even know what I wanted. I had hoped that spending these next few months with Gran would help me discover my path. I knew my parents considered me to be an entitled millennial, and that at my age I should have my act together. When they'd been my age they were already married and working as archaeologists. All I had to show for my twenty-seven years on earth was a business degree from a community college and a string of failed relationships.

He named a figure. I stared at him. He said, "That's pounds not dollars. The amount will be even higher when translated into American dollars."

I narrowed my eyes. "Is that the amount for all four shops?"

"No. Just the building that houses Cardinal Woolsey's and the living accommodation above it."

With that kind of money I could travel, buy a nice condo pretty much anywhere in the world, and do whatever I wanted without having to worry about money for a little while. I admit, it was intoxicating.

But I couldn't make this kind of decision without thinking about it carefully. And, what he didn't know was that I could consult my grandmother. Also, even if my mother hadn't been named as the beneficiary, I wanted her opinion. "I need to get hold of my mother."

"Of course. I hope we can move on this quickly."

"What about the other shops?"

"They've all agreed. But I want all of them or none, you understand." Great. Now he was putting pressure on me as the last holdout.

He handed me a business card. "Talk it all over with your mother and anyone else you like. Get back to me when you've made up your mind. Don't leave it too long, though, I have a notoriously short attention span."

I could believe that. He'd made short work of his quiche and was even now gesturing for the bill. Mary Watt saw him and brought the bill over herself. "Why Mr. Hatfield. How nice to see you again."

"Miss Watt. Always a pleasure. You know I'd come a long way for your delicious home cooking."

She giggled and blushed like a schoolgirl. To me she said, "I'm glad you've met Mr. Hatfield."

He put down cash then stood and said, "I'll leave you two ladies to chat then." And to me he said, "We'll be in touch."

I appreciated that he was leaving Miss Watt and me alone for a few moments. I asked, "Has he really talked to you about buying the tea shop?"

"Oh yes. And, at our age, how long do we want to continue working so hard? Of course, we love the tea shop, and would never want to lose it, but he promises to continue to run it as is."

"It almost seems too good to be true."

"I know. He's willing to pay top dollar, too. We could finally retire and spend some time in the South of France. I've always wanted to spend the winter somewhere warm, but the shop does tie one down. The people who own the gift shop are very keen. They've only had it a couple of years and I think it's more work than they realized."

I knew that the Wrights were keen, as their son had told me so. "Was Gran really ready to sell?"

Miss Watt glanced around, possibly to make sure Richard Hatfield had left. She said, "I'm not sure, honestly. She seemed reluctant, though we all tried to convince her it was for the best. He wants all the shops, you see, or none of them." She began to stack the plates. "Naturally, we shared the same worry, that he wouldn't respect the tradition, and the fact that these little businesses have been here for so long, but he does. We all agreed. Except your grandmother."

"Except my grandmother?" Richard Hatfield had suggested she was anxious to sign the deal. Now, Miss Watt seemed to be telling me something different.

"I'm not saying she was against the deal, exactly, but she wasn't keen. I think she planned to discuss it all with you."

Well, if my grandmother hadn't been in a hurry, I needn't be in one either. Alive or undead, I still wanted her advice.

I came out of Elderflower and as I turned to go back into the yarn shop, Detective Inspector Ian Chisholm was walking toward me. I waited until he reached where I was standing.

He said, "It's nice to see the store open again. I hope you're thinking of staying?"

With the very generous offer from Richard Hatfield still rattling around in my head, I was leaning toward leaving Oxford, knowing Cardinal Woolsey's would be safe. "I'll continue running the shop until I make a decision."

"That seems like a good idea. As a matter of fact, I was going to pop in and buy my auntie another skein of that wool. She's run out."

He was disturbingly attractive standing outside, the breeze just lifting his hair as though running her hands through it. He made a motion as though to usher me inside but I stopped him with a hand on his arm. "I heard there was a break-in recently, would you know anything about that?"

He glanced toward the shop window, where Nyx was still curled up, looking particularly adorable, watching us through eyes only half open. If she was my familiar, as Gran had suggested, she was a lazy one. A couple walked by arm in arm and the girl said, "Oh, look at that cat. Could he be any cuter?" And, letting go of her guy, she slipped out her phone and took a snap. And, before my eyes, she tapped something and uploaded the photo, presumably to some social media site.

Ian, also watched. "You should put something with your shop name on it. That cat's giving you a free advertising opportunity."

"That's a great idea." I was the one who'd been to

business college, while the cop was giving me marketing advice.

He said, "A break in at Cardinal Woolsey's?" Okay, he'd taken off his marketing hat and put his copper hat back on.

"Yes. That's what my assistant said. But Gran never mentioned it in our emails. I wondered if she didn't want to worry me."

"But you are worried."

"I'm staying here, as well as running the shop, I'd feel more comfortable if I knew that whoever broke into the shop had been caught. That's all. I'm not sure Gran ever reported it, but I imagine if there was one break-in in the area there might have been several?"

He glanced around the windows and at the door in a professional way. "It's easy enough to break into, but the question is, why would anyone choose this place? You wouldn't expect to find much in the till and the merchandise isn't the sort of stuff that you fence."

It was exactly what I'd thought. Who in their right mind knocked over a knitting shop?

"I don't really deal in theft and burglary, but I'll see what I can find out for you."

"Unofficially?"

He looked at me, his eyes slightly narrowed, "Why does it matter?"

I didn't want to draw attention to the shop for about a dozen sharp-toothed reasons. I said, "I suppose it's silly, but if it gets out that we were broken into once, maybe the wrong sort of people would get ideas that there's something here worth stealing."

"Is there?"

"No. Most of our customers pay by credit card or debit and at the end of the day we take what cash there is to the bank. We only keep a small float in the till. And as you said yourself, the contents of the shop wouldn't be valuable to anyone but a knitter."

"Not the most larcenous of people, are they?" A pair of sweet-looking old ladies were even now entering the shop.

"Exactly."

"Well, I'll see what I can find out for you." He leaned in toward me and his eyes twinkled disturbingly. "Unofficially."

Once more I had the intriguing notion that he was flirting with me. It had been a long time since I had excited so much male admiration. The air in Oxford must be good for me.

A group of four more ladies went into the shop. I said, "I'd better get in. We're having a very busy day."

He didn't follow me and I didn't have time to pay him any more attention as the little shop was buzzing with customers. While some had come with knitting purchases in mind, it was clear that many others simply wanted to pay their respects to Gran. I definitely got the sense that there was some nosiness among knitters who wanted to know whether the shop was going to stay open.

Two estate agents came through, obviously more interested in the dimensions of the shop than what it sold. Both gave me their sincerest condolences as well as their business cards, and let me know that they worked in the area and would be only too happy to help if I planned to let the shop or if the family had thoughts of selling the property. My poor gran was barely gone and the vultures were pecking at her remains.

Even though I knew they were only trying to do their jobs, I felt suddenly protective of this little shop, and all its customers. The four ladies had driven in from another town after they saw on social media that the shop had reopened. They were part of a knitting circle and always shopped at Cardinal Woolsey's. "We're so pleased you're open again. We've got to get started on our Christmas projects."

Over the course of the day, I received condolence cards, baked cookies and cakes, even a jar of homemade jam. And each person had a story about my grandmother; perhaps she had taught them to knit, or helped their aged, arthritic mother find a project she could manage. She'd given advice on colors and patterns, ordered in specialty products, donated to various charitable causes. I had always known my grandmother as the kind and warm woman who had given me a home while my parents were off on digs, but now I saw her as a business woman in a small community, who had provided countless hours of pleasure to her customers. Her passing would leave a great many holes in a great many lives.

As one, the people who brought in cards and food and, most important of all, their memories and stories, wanted to be reassured that Cardinal Woolsey's would continue to operate. I didn't want to lie to these people, but I honestly didn't know what I was going to do. I gave them the same stock answer that I had given to the detective. I was running the shop for now, and I would let them know when I had made a decision about the future.

One of the ladies who came in to express her sorrow did a double take when she saw Rosemary. She lowered her voice, even though my assistant was busy in the corner helping another customer. She said, "So you've hired Rosemary back?"

"Hired her back?" The surprise must have showed in my tone for she said, "She wasn't here the last time I came to the shop and your grandmother said that she no longer worked here. I got the impression she'd fired her. She's been here for years, so, something must have happened."

Rosemary hadn't said anything to me about not working here anymore. But then I remembered how strangely she'd acted when I first phoned her, and she didn't have a key for the door. Hmm.

However, I didn't know what I would've done without Rosemary today. She knew where everything went, knew about half of the customers personally, and seemed to be doing an excellent job. Still, I made a mental note to keep an eye on her.

Later, I was helping two women choose colors for a sweater when one put her hand on her friend's arm and gestured with her chin toward the door. "Oh my, he can knit me a twin set any day." I glanced back to see Ian Chisholm had entered the shop. He looked particularly manly surrounded by baskets of wool and every other customer in the shop at that time was female. I could actually hear the buzz as the women noted his presence.

I doubted he was aware of it: he had the tag from a skein of knitting wool, and glanced around, helplessly. I excused myself, walked over. "Is that your Aunt's wool?"

"Yes. How do you keep track of all this stuff?" He looked baffled at the numbers of baskets and wool-stocked shelves confronting him.

"There's a trick to it," I said. "Let me take a look at that." I checked the tag. The wool he was looking for was the same blue that sweet old vampire had used to knit my sweater. In fact, she had used the last of our stock. I told him I could order it for him and have it here within the week and he said that was fine. I went behind the cash desk and retrieved the special order book.

I felt a bit silly asking him for his phone number. He hesitated, as we both knew that I had his business card. "I'll give you my personal mobile number." I may have blushed a little as I wrote it down. Especially when he said, "That number will reach me day or night."

When we closed the shop that evening, I had to hold the door open and usher the last customers out. In all the times I had helped my grandmother in the shop, I never remembered a busier day. Rosemary pushed a hand through her hair and said, "Phew. I was run off my feet."

"I think a lot of people came in to pay their respects."

"And they all spent a bit of dosh," she reminded me.

"That they did. And that reminds me, I need to get the cash to the bank." If there had been a break-in, then thieves must work in the area.

"I can do that for you. I always used to do the night deposit for your grandmother."

I didn't want to trust her with a bag of cash. Besides, there was an unsavory looking character hanging around outside the shop. He looked to be in his late twenties, with a tattoo of a pit bull, I think it was, up the side of his neck. He was smoking a rolled up cigarette and kept glancing into the shop. His face reminded me of a pit bull's, even without the tattoo. I didn't want Rosemary walking past him with the deposit. I said, "I'll do it myself, tonight. You get on home."

She shrugged and said, "Please yourself. See you tomorrow."

Even if my grandmother had fired her, we both knew I couldn't have managed today without her help. "Yes. I'll see you tomorrow."

She gathered her bag and left. When she got outside, the pit bull guy walked up to her. Was he panhandling? But soon it was clear they knew each other and walked off together. It looked as though they were arguing. I didn't need special powers to figure out that this must be Randolph.

I went to the cash register and began counting up

the money, and reconciling it with the sales. It was part of the job I'd always enjoyed. I wasn't good with wool, or knitting, but I was very good with numbers. I knew that Gran would be pleased when I told her how well we'd done today and especially how many people had spoken so kindly of her. I only wished I knew how to get hold of her. Rafe had a mobile. Perhaps we could set Gran up with one as well.

After making certain pit-bull tattoo boy was gone, I carried the deposit up to the bank unmolested and returned to the shop. Nyx woke from her latest nap and meowed pathetically. I felt let down, too, after that wonderful day. Now the shop seemed quiet and empty and dark. I took Nyx upstairs and fed her a tin of the tuna she liked. I'd try and find my grandmother. How hard could it be? I'd seen the vampires go down that trapdoor. I decided to investigate.

THIRTEEN

I LEFT MY sweater on, hoping I'd get a chance to show it off to Clara. But I changed my skirt for jeans and found a flashlight. Having finished her tuna, Nyx seemed inclined to accompany me and, truth to tell, I was glad of the company. I had no idea what lay beneath that trapdoor, but I knew there were tunnels underneath Oxford and subterranean tunnels made me think of rats.

Theoretically, vampires were more dangerous, but I was frankly more frightened of rats.

In fact, when I walked through the shop and into the back room to where that trapdoor was, I hesitated. I had been given no invitation to, "drop by anytime," and yet here I was thinking I would be welcome. My hand went to my mouth and I began to gnaw my thumbnail. Nyx tapped her paw on the door. It made me smile, and also realize that if they were busy, or still sleeping, I could come back up.

"Here we go," I said and reached down and pulled up the lid of the trapdoor. I peered down into inky darkness. If I hadn't seen a dozen vampires climb down there one by one I would have believed there was nothing down there. I clicked on the flashlight and trained the light into the gaping hole.

There were stairs there. Very old looking wooden stairs, but what they led to I couldn't tell without climbing down. Once more, I was reminded that the vampires hadn't invited me to come visiting, but then they had seemed so friendly at the knitting club and surely Gran would want to know how I'd made out on my first day running the shop without her.

I held on with one hand and, using the flashlight to guide me, I began to walk down the stairs. When my head was below the level of the shop floor the atmosphere changed. The air smelled thicker, musty and slightly damp. I had no idea what I'd find once I got to the bottom of the stairs. Stacked coffins?

I reached the bottom of the staircase and found myself on the stone walkway of a tunnel. I looked over the edge and saw water moving very slowly several feet below my feet. I couldn't see light whether I looked behind or in front of me. I shivered, wondering if I should go back upstairs, but Nyx trotted on ahead of me and I refused to act more scared than a kitten.

The stone walls of the tunnel were dry. The cobbles were uneven beneath my feet but perfectly sound. I could hear my own breathing and the scuff of my feet on the ground. Fortunately, there were no sounds of scurrying.

If I hadn't been looking for it, I would have missed the old, wooden door set into the wall.

The door looked ancient, with a metal handle that appeared untouched by human hands for centuries. I'd have guessed it to be some sort of storage vault but, knowing my knitting friends were down here somewhere, I decided to start here. It was just after seven in the evening and I hoped I wasn't rousing them too early as I banged on the door with my fist. I waited. Nothing happened. No one answered.

Nyx stood beside me looking up expectantly.

I was about to turn back when I got the strangest feeling I was being watched. Next thing I knew, the door opened soundlessly on well-oiled hinges.

Rafe stood at the door, eyebrows raised. He did not look particularly pleased to see me. "Lucy, this is a surprise."

He'd probably been perfecting this brand of sarcasm for half a millennium and he was very effective with it. I immediately felt that I was acting inappropriately and trespassing, which was rich, given that their home was beneath the shop that now belonged to me. I reminded myself that I was, in essence, their landlady and as such perfectly in my rights to tour the premises. "I was hoping to speak to my grandmother."

I could tell he was about to fob me off when I heard Gran say from behind him, "Is that Lucy?" And then she was there, behind his shoulder, saying, "Come in, my love. Tell me all about your first day. I so wanted to pop up and see how you were doing, but Sylvia told me I couldn't." Her lips pursed and I imagined harsh words had been exchanged.

There wasn't much Rafe could do once I'd been so enthusiastically invited in. With the barest lifting of his shoulders he stepped back and opened the door wide. I stepped in expecting to see stacked coffins and perhaps old barrels and coils of rope, dust and dirt and, if I'm honest, rat droppings. The sight that met my eyes was enough to make my jaw drop.

I'd attended Phantom of the Opera in London's West End with my grandmother back when I was a teenager, and if the vampires had used the same set designer I wouldn't have been a bit surprised. Their lair was voluptuous, with red velvet settees and deep, comfortable-looking chairs and two couches set in a circle. The light came from crystal chandeliers and ornate lamps. On the walls were tapestry hangings that could have hung in the Louvre.

While I was looking around, Sylvia came in wearing a silk designer robe in black and gold. She yawned and sank into one of the ornate chairs, looking right at home.

And the paintings! I'm no expert, but the heavy framed artworks looked original and expensive. I walked right up to one that did look familiar. "Is that a Van Gogh?" It depicted a vase of sunflowers, but not one I ever remembered seeing before.

Rafe came up behind me. "Yes. I picked it up in Paris, years ago. His work wasn't popular at the time, but I thought he had something."

"You thought he had something," I said faintly.

"If you're interested in Impressionists, I have a

private collection at my house."

I turned to him in surprise. "Your house? But don't you live here?"

"No. I have a place near Woodstock, but I've been spending more time here lately."

Sylvia snorted and said, "For one very obvious reason."

I glanced at her and waited for more, but Gran said, "Now, Sylvia. Leave them be."

I glanced swiftly at Rafe but he appeared oblivious. He ushered me toward the seating area. "Come, your grandmother's been most anxious to hear about your first day." I wondered if they'd needed brute force to keep her out of the shop in broad daylight. Knowing Gran the answer was probably yes.

Through an archway I glimpsed a very modern looking series of stainless steel refrigerators. I had a feeling that the blood bank was kept here.

Incongruously, a big-screen television sat in one corner and on top of a gorgeous antique desk was a top-of-the-line computer. As I walked to the conversation circle, my feet sank into the most luxurious of Persian carpets. I didn't see rows of coffins but there were several arches leading from this main chamber and I imagined the bedrooms lay back there.

Nyx brushed against my ankles. I bent down and picked her up, thinking she might feel frightened. Perhaps I was the one feeling a bit frightened. I hadn't brought the garlic or the holy water or the crucifix with me. All I had by way of vampire deterrents was the silver cross on a sterling chain around my neck. I suspected, against a nest of hungry vampires, one silver chain and one feisty kitten wouldn't be much protection.

But there was Gran, looking much more like my grandmother than a vampire. And so pleased to see me. "Come and sit down," she said.

She led me forward to a deep red velvet couch. The color of blood, I realized, as I sank into it. "Rafe? Have we refreshment we can offer Lucy?"

"Of course," he said, his urbanity restored. He walked to a beautiful and intricately carved cabinet and opened the door. There was a set of crystal glasses, and a single bottle of Harvey's Bristol Cream. I began to feel less frightened as Rafe and I exchanged a glance. They stocked her favorite sherry, which suggested that my grandmother had been a visitor here when she was still human.

He poured me a glass and brought it over. Gran said, "I'd love to join you, but my stomach hasn't been quite right since my change." She lowered her voice on the last word and in a different context I thought she could've been referring to the menopause. But this had been a more dramatic change of life.

I raised my glass in a silent toast and sipped the thick, sweet liquid. Then I set the glass down and turned to her. "We had the most amazing day. So many of your customers came in and told stories of you, of how you taught them to knit, or ordered something special for them. In a couple of cases a mother and daughter came in together and you'd taught them both. Your customers loved you."

I offered her the stack of condolence cards and notes I'd brought with me. She read each of them with pleasure, reading choice bits aloud. I didn't want to spoil the moment, but I had to ask about Rosemary.

While I recounted my conversation with the customer who had thought Rosemary had been fired, Gran shook her head, looking mystified.

Sylvia went into the kitchen. I heard a fridge opening and then in a moment she returned carrying two insulated mugs, the kind available in most coffee store chains. She handed one to Gran and sat across from me, folding her legs beneath her. It was strange, looking at these women, who had clearly only just woken, drinking what, in the world above, would likely be coffee.

My grandmother drank hers gratefully and seemed to find the taste perfectly palatable. Clara wandered in, also yawning. She wore a thick pink terrycloth robe with the name of a high-end hotel and spa embroidered on the lapel. On her feet were cozy knitted pink slippers.

When she saw me, she cried out with delight. "Oh, you wore the sweater. My dear, it looks beautiful on you." She waved her hands up and down, indicating that I should stand up. I did and immediately turned in a circle so she could admire her handiwork. She beamed. "I can't believe how well it turned out."

"I'm thrilled with it. And, you wouldn't believe the number of customers today who came in and saw me in this sweater and then wanted to knit one just like it."

She chuckled, in a slightly superior way. "Well,

they won't be able to knit one just like it because I designed it for you."

"I know. It's like wearable art. But, we did find a much simpler pattern and sold half a dozen of them today, plus all the wool." I said to Gran, "I'll have to put in a new order tonight if we're going to keep up."

"What was the day's take?" she asked. I told her and she clapped her hands in delight. "We usually only see days like that in November and December, as knitters prepare for Christmas."

We'd gone off the topic of the possibly-fired assistant but now I brought it up again.

Gran looked puzzled. "Really? The woman said Rosemary didn't work there anymore?" She rubbed her temples as though she could massage her memory back into place. Clara said gently, "Don't you remember, Agnes? You were very upset. You told us at one of the knitting club meetings that you'd had to let your assistant go."

She shook her head. "No. I don't remember that. Why would I fire Rosemary? She'd worked for me for years."

"You didn't give the details. I think you still had some loyalty to her and refused to gossip behind her back." Clara sounded disappointed, as though she would've liked a bit of gossip with her knitting.

I wished she'd spilled the beans too so I'd know whether I should look for a new assistant. "I've asked Rosemary to come in again. She was so efficient today, and, of course, knows half the clientele and where everything is. I carried today's cash to the bank myself, and I'm not giving her a door key." I felt that I was doing what I could to minimize any damage the woman could cause. But I knew I'd be keeping my eye on her.

Rafe said, "Agnes fired Rosemary because she was stealing."

"Really?"

"To feed the son's drug habit. He's the only person she cares about more than herself."

Gran said, "Poor Rosemary. That son's been a problem for years. I don't remember firing her, but if she was stealing, I'd have had to."

"How did you know?" Clara asked Rafe, clearly miffed that Gran had told him and not her.

"You'd be surprised at some of the people I know in this town. And people talk."

I sipped more sherry wondering whether I could smuggle in a bottle of something I liked better for future meetings, assuming I was ever invited back. When I lifted my hand, Gran said, "Good. You've found my old ruby ring."

I felt immediately guilty. "Was it okay for me to wear it? It was sitting in your jewelry box and I wore it for good luck today. Do you want it back?"

"No. I want you to wear it. It will warn you when you're in danger. Wear it always."

Oh, that got my attention. "How does it warn me, Gran?"

"It will feel hot on your hand, and sometimes, if you look carefully, there will be a slight glow that only you can see."

Oh, boy. "That exact thing happened when Rosemary came in this morning." I wondered the unthinkable. Could Rosemary have been so angry with Gran for firing her, and for suggesting her son was no good, that she'd killed her? Now I'd let the woman back into the shop and was paying her! *Way to go, Lucy.*

Gran said, "I always trusted Rosemary, but if she set off the ring you must be very careful."

My thumb crept to my mouth. "Should I tell her not to come back?" She'd been such a lifesaver today; I dreaded having to manage alone.

Gran looked to Rafe who was heading toward the computer desk. I felt irked. I hadn't asked him. Why did they all treat him as though he knew everything? It was very annoying. Especially as he did seem to know everything. *I thought Van Gogh had something.* Honestly!

Rafe considered and said, "So long as you keep an eye on her and are warned she isn't your friend, I think you'll be all right. There are customers in and out of that shop all day long. What can she do?"

Since I agreed with him, his advice was good, which annoyed me, as I'd planned to do the opposite of whatever he decreed. "There's something else I want to discuss with you," I said. Rafe had sat down, but hearing my serious tone, he turned in his seat to look at me. Gran, Sylvia and Clara were gathered around. Nyx curled up in my lap. "A man came into the shop today. His name is Richard Hatfield." I looked to see if my grandmother knew the name but she merely nodded encouragingly, waiting for me to go on.

"He says he wants to buy your shop. In fact, he's planning to buy all the shops in our row. He promised to preserve them as they are. He said that you had already agreed to sell to him and simply hadn't had time to sign a contract before…" My words petered out. I could not finish that sentence.

Gran looked around at the other occupants of the room and said, in a puzzled tone, "I had agreed to sell the shop?" She shook her head. "I don't remember agreeing to that. Of course, I can't remember much of anything from the period leading up to my death, but I would never sell that shop." She turned to me and reached for my hand. One day, I was certain I'd become used to her cool touch. "I intended for you to have it."

"Then he's lying," I said.

Rafe spoke. "Be careful around him, Lucy. I've had plenty of time to learn to judge humans and that one's a bad man pretending to be everyone's friend. He's the kind who'd kill to get what he wanted, all the while smiling into your face. The shop belongs to you now, it's up to you to see it doesn't fall into the wrong hands."

Again with the bossiness. I thought it was time I told him I made my own decisions. I wasn't one of his vampire minions. "It's a knitting shop, not a nuclear arsenal. I think I should explore all the options." To Gran I asked the question that had been bothering me. "Why did you leave the shop to me? And not my mother?"

She smiled. "Your mother is my daughter, and I love her. But she's much more interested in digging up history then taking care of Cardinal Woolsey's. She'd no more run a knitting shop then she'd fly to the moon. You, on the other hand, I've always known you belong here." She said this with such certainty, and here I was miserably unsure about what I wanted to do with my life. Running a knitting shop had never been in my plans. I didn't want to hurt her feelings, but I felt I had to say something. "Gran, I'm not sure I'm cut out to run the shop."

Her cool palm patted my hand. "My darling girl, you have a destiny. You come from a proud and distinguished line of witches. You could no more reject your fate than you could—"

"Fly to the moon," I finished the sentence for her.

She chuckled. "Exactly."

"I don't even know how to be a witch." Never mind that I wasn't going to take the word of a freshly-turned vampire as solid gold career counseling. "Shouldn't I have known?"

Gran looked sad. "Imagine if you were born to sing and every time you opened your mouth and sang a note, you were criticized or scolded. What would happen?"

Memories began to creep over me, like mist over an early morning meadow. Times when I'd told Mom about my vivid dreams and she'd told me to get my head out of the clouds. When I'd felt things and tried to explain them and she'd said I was being foolish. "I'd sing very softly in the shower."

"Exactly. And your voice would remain weak and untrained. Your parents meant well, but they stifled that part of you, as if they could keep the magic from appearing. Now that you're free and encouraged, your powers are rushing to be used. Can't you feel it? Nyx certainly can. Apart from the ring glowing, have you had other signs?"

"I did have some kind of electricity zapping out of my fingertips when I was angry."

"Excellent. All you need is practice. And I've preserved the grimoire for you, our family's book of spells. Everything you need to know is in that book."

"That's great, Gran. There's just one tiny problem."

She nodded her head. "I know, it's surrounded by a protection spell. You can't open the book until you work out how to release the spell."

"Okay, I guess there are two tiny problems. I have to come up with a spell, and the book is missing."

The four-hundred-year-old teenager, Hester, wandered in, yawning. She wore plaid pajamas and a black hoodie instead of a robe. I wondered how her life had been cut short, so young. She glanced around, and the habitual pout settled on her face.

"What's going on? I slept in. Someone should've woken me. How come I always miss everything?" She glanced at me with suspicion. "What's she doing here?"

I wondered how the others put up with her, but

Clara merely said, "You haven't missed anything, dear. And Lucy owns the shop now. We'll be seeing a lot of her. Perhaps you should knit her a pair of those slippers you do so well."

The girl rolled her eyes and said, "Yeah. I'll get right on it."

"Very difficult, the teenage years," Clara said in a stage whisper. Of course, most teenagers would grow out of their awkward adolescence but I suspected this one was stuck in teenaged torment for eternity.

I stood up, lifting the cat as I did so. "I should get back. I've got to get our order in if we're going to have enough stock to keep up with all this business."

Gran rose to say good-bye and hugged me. "Thank you for bringing me these cards. They'll cheer me up when I feel blue."

I wondered how a collection of condolence cards for your own death could possibly be cheering, but I kept that thought to myself. As I headed for the heavy oak door Rafe stood. "I'll see you back to the shop."

I looked back at him in surprise. It wasn't exactly a long journey. Something in his expression told me not to argue with him. He reached around me and did some complicated thing with the door handle and then turned it and opened the door smoothly.

We entered back into the tunnel under the shop and headed for the stairs. "You shouldn't come down here alone. Call me next time and I'll escort you."

I was genuinely puzzled and must've looked it, because he said, "We aren't the only creatures you could run into down here. It's best if I come with you."

If I was going to sleep tonight I really didn't want to know what other creatures might be beneath the floorboards so I simply nodded. I climbed up the stairs, very conscious of him following behind. I'd left the trap door into the back part of the shop open so that I could easily get back again. I climbed up into the shop and turned to thank him but he was already standing beside me. "It's important to keep this trap door closed at all times. Normally, we keep it locked. For all our safety."

Then he knelt to the ground and showed me the ingenious mechanism that locked it. He explained that a similar lever operated from the other side so it could be opened from above and below. I thought he'd go then but he said, "Your grandmother had no intention of selling her shop. I didn't say anything in front of her, because I don't like to remind her that she's missing some vital parts of her memory, but I can assure you she said no time and time again to that pushy Richard Hatfield."

"Really? That's not the story he told. In fact, Miss Watt thought my grandmother was leaning toward selling, and the Wrights definitely thought she was going to sell. It seems they're all in agreement."

He shook his head sharply. "The other three owners all have their own reasons for wanting that money. But your grandmother was determined to hold onto this for you."

I raised my eyebrows in a skeptical fashion. "And for you."

He acknowledged the truth of that statement with a slight nod of his head.

"I thought she might be interested, since he insists that he will leave the shops as they are. He seems to have a nostalgic regard for them."

Rafe made a rude sound and uttered a phrase I'd never heard before. "What did you say?"

"You have sharp ears. I said *Bovis Stercus*. It's Latin for the excrement of a bull."

I rolled my eyes. "Only in Oxford." Although he probably learned the phrase in ancient Rome back when they spoke Latin every day. "One of you is obviously lying. How on earth do I figure out which one? You both have something to gain."

"Press Richard Hatfield for a promise in writing that he won't change these old shops and see what he says."

I felt proud of myself, because I had asked Richard Hatfield that very question. It was with a hint of pride that I said, "I did ask him. He he's only buying them for an investment."

He nodded with satisfaction. "Oh, it's an investment all right. He plans to knock the interiors together and turn the ground floor into a top end restaurant. The flats upstairs will be gutted and turned into luxury apartments."

"How do you know?"

"I have sources. I've seen the plans. I can show them to you. Don't be naïve. That man has no intention of preserving these old shops. Putting together a piece of property like this is worth a fortune to a developer."

"I suppose."

He looked at me as though he could see right inside my head. "You're struggling. You've had a lot to take in in a short period of time. Losing your grandmother, finding out her death wasn't an accident, learning that you have powers of your own—"

When I shook my head and held up my hands as if I could physically push his words away, he smiled slightly. "And on top of that you've now got a developer offering you a deal that is much too good to be true. Take my advice as someone who is a great deal older than you are, don't rush into anything. Take your time. Things will work out." His words were spoken softly and with such an understanding that I felt the tightness in my shoulders begin to relax.

"You look tired. Why don't you try to get to bed early?"

"I will. As soon as I've made the order."

I thought he'd say more but he simply said, "Good night." And then he unlocked the trapdoor and disappeared into the tunnels. I heard the unmistakable click of the lock, and pulled the rug back to hide the door.

I headed into the shop, Nyx at my heels. I did feel tired, and a bit overwhelmed by all of this. But, if I was going to run Cardinal Woolsey's then I needed stock. If we had many more days like today, and no new stock, the shelves would be bare. I owed it to my grandmother to do as good a job of running her shop as I could.

I went upstairs to get my laptop. I would place the

order online, using the notes I'd made in grandmother's book. If I stayed, I would computerize the system. For now, the big leather-bound book would do. As my grandmother always said, the system had been working fine for the past fifty years. No doubt, it would continue to work flawlessly for another few months.

I didn't know when she had last put in an order, and what quantities she usually ordered, so I paged back a few months, getting a sense of how often she put in orders and what was most popular. Rosemary and Gran had both made notes, but the last one from Rosemary was nearly three months ago.

It was quiet, with only the scrape of my pen on paper and the tap of my fingers on my computer keys. Nyx jumped lightly onto the counter and amused herself by trying to walk across my keyboard while I was typing.

I was trying to decipher my grandmother's handwriting. This must've been one of her last orders that she put in the book and that hadn't yet gone to our supplier. I was bent over, squinting at her spidery handwriting. Was that two skeins of the hand spun angora or twelve?"

Nyx sat on the counter, also with her head bent over the book as though she, too, were reading it, when she suddenly stiffened, raised her head and looked behind me. Her eyes grew round.

I heard a noise behind me and grabbed up the only weapon I could see, an umbrella tucked under the counter. I swung around, holding the umbrella like machete, ready to do battle, feeling the energy humming in my fingertips.

Gran jumped back. "Oh, dear. I've startled you."

I put the umbrella down with a shaky laugh. "Sorry. Knowing you were attacked in here has me a little on edge."

"I'm pleased to see you on your guard, but your magic is stronger than an old umbrella. Come on. I'm giving you your first lesson."

"In self-defense?"

"In magic."

"But I can't find the book of spells."

She waved that away. "Books aren't everything. Now, where shall we begin?"

She walked around the shop, sticking her nose in random baskets, reminding me of my cat. I thought she was enjoying being back in the shop, feeling triumph at how much of the stock had sold today.

"The best help you can give me is to help me figure out what to order."

"But first, I want you to reorganize the shop."

I couldn't have heard her correctly. "But you have a system that works."

"We can put everything back again. But let's have some fun."

Reordering the shop and then putting everything back again did not sound like fun. I'd been on my feet all day. We'd be here all night if we followed her crazy idea.

She winked at me and then, making a circular

motion with her index finger, said, "Blues switch with reds." Before my astonished gaze, balls of wool in those two colors rose out of their baskets and floated across the room, neatly missing each other before swapping places.

"How did I never know you were a witch?" I whispered.

"Your mother wouldn't allow me to speak of it. She made me promise before she allowed you to visit me." She sighed. "She's one of us, too, but she won't acknowledge her power. Instead, she suppresses it. I worry about her. She's made herself vulnerable. Still, she works in remote areas. That should keep her safe."

Safe from what, I wondered, but I was more interested in balls of wool that could fly on their own. "How did you do that?" *And can I try?*

"You must concentrate and picture exactly what you wish to happen. Then say it out loud."

"Do I make the circular finger movement the way you did?"

"That was for show, but go ahead."

I breathed deeply, pictured exactly what I wanted. I waved my index finger in a circle too, because it looked so witchy. "Everything in alphabetical order," I said with as much confidence as I could. That feeling started up in my fingers again and, less shockingly this time, I saw blue-white electricity zap through my fingertips. I was thrilled when balls of wool and twisted skeins rose up from the baskets and began to parade and waltz through the air.

I watched in excitement as the Aran wool swapped places with the Alpaca. The wools were floating nicely, taking their places, when the buttons floated off the wall racks. The crochet hooks headed toward them. But I hadn't meant the notions to rearrange themselves, only the wool.

Nyx had watched wide-eyed. Now, as I fretted about my mistake, the wafting wools, cavorting crochet hooks and bouncing buttons wavered. The cat jumped to the ground as the wools began to float downward, like balloons losing their air. She jumped up on her hind legs and swiped at a ball of purple mohair, then pounced on a glittery skein of gold chunky yarn. "No," I cried as the entire stock of the knitting shop turned into a treasure trove of cat toys.

"Concentrate," Gran said. "Try again."

"Up, up, up," I said aloud, spiraling my finger upwards. Obediently, the balls and skeins, the buttons and needles rose in the air. The chunky wool under Nyx's paw tugged itself out of her grasp and as it rose, she pounced, all kitten and no sense, and then hung on, rising with the wool. I couldn't laugh, couldn't lose my concentration or Nyx could be hurt, so I kept my mind on everything arranged alphabetically. When the gold chunky yarn floated into a basket, taking the cat with it, Nyx seemed delighted, and rolled around and then popped her head over the edge. A piece of gold wool hung over her ear like a tassel.

"You did it," Gran said, clapping her hands.

"I did!"

"Now, try again."

This time, I said, "Wools only," and ordered them in rainbow order. ROYGBIV. It worked well except for the variegated yarns, which floated aimlessly up and down the rainbow until I sent them to their own basket.

We'd returned everything when Sylvia came to collect Gran for their midnight outing. She hugged me before she left and said, "If I can't teach you to knit, at least I can teach you to be a very good witch."

What did it say about me that knitting spells was easier than crafting a simple scarf?

FOURTEEN

I WENT DOWN to the shop early Saturday morning, feeling excited about my newfound powers, determined to find that grimoire and hopeful of having another sales day as good as yesterday's.

I wore the same blue sweater that had generated so many sales yesterday, assuming I'd have a new set of customers today to wow with my wearable art. However, when I entered the shop my foot bumped yet another bag containing yet another sweater. I recognized the wool, it was the chunky alpaca in purple. The garment was gorgeous with a scoopy neck and big sleeves that folded over into pretty cuffs. I'd worn black trousers and a white shirt so I simply took off the blue sweater and slipped the purple one over my head. I pulled my hair out from under the collar and let it swing loose around my shoulders.

I took the blue sweater I'd been wearing yesterday, placed it on a hanger, and displayed it on the wall. I had a feeling that very soon I was going to have my walls covered with examples of the most amazing knitted items that ingenious and very nimble fingers could devise. I strutted down the center of the shop as though I were a top model and this was my runway. I struck a pose in front of Nyx and said, "I am the Naomi Campbell of the cardigan." Nyx yawned and bathed me in tuna breath.

Rosemary arrived a few minutes late this morning but I didn't chide her as her eyes looked puffy, either from lack of sleep or from crying. "Is everything all right?"

Her expression turned belligerent. "Why wouldn't it be?"

Okay then, I'd keep my sympathy to myself. Fortunately there wasn't time for more, as our first customer arrived. She pointed to the sweater on the wall, the one I'd been wearing yesterday. "I saw that on your Facebook page. It looks so nice, I decided to knit myself something for a change. I'm always knitting for other people, but I want that sweater for myself. It gets cold in the lab where I work."

I had to regretfully explain that all the wool had sold out yesterday, but I had a new order coming in that should arrive Tuesday. She looked at the sweater I was wearing. "What about that one? Do you have the wool for that?"

Oh we had lots of the chunky alpaca in stock. I wondered if it was Gran's idea to kit me out in a sweater that promoted the wools we had most of in stock, and I silently congratulated her.

Of course, I knew so little about knitting that I turned the customer over to Rosemary, who managed to

rally and began digging through the patterns finding
something that would approximate what I was wearing,
while the woman happily collected balls of purple yarn.

If the day wasn't quite as busy as the one before, it
was still a happening place. I'd just accepted a jar of
homemade quince jelly from a longtime customer with
fond memories of my grandmother, and added it to the
collection of cards and small gifts, when my nostrils
twitched. I smelled a combination of burned lavender
and sage. I glanced around and found myself
confronting an interesting looking woman.

She was about my own age, with long black hair
that she had styled into a single braid that hung over one
shoulder. Her bangs were streaked with bright red and
pink and purple and she carried the multi-colours
through a single stripe of hair. Her eyes were round and
bright, almost like black buttons, her lips were painted
the same red as her hair and her clothing style was what
I would call dramatic. Black boots, a full black skirt,
and a loose woven jacket in red and black. But what
caught my eye was her necklace. Hanging at the end of
a gold chain was a ruby set in gold filigree. It looked
exactly like my ring.

As she walked towards me her high-heeled boots
tapped like snapping fingers. "Are you Lucy Swift?"

"I am." I was certain I had never seen this woman in
my life, so I wondered how she was knew me.

"I'm Violet Weeks."

"Violet Weeks was the cousin I'd never known I
had. The one who had supposedly taken care of Gran's
funeral. "So you're real?" I believe I've mentioned I

blurt out stupid things when I'm nervous.

She looked taken aback by my question but decided to be amused. She lifted her hands and held them out like a magician who's just conjured a rabbit out of a hat. Silver bracelets jangled on her wrists and she had more rings on than fingers to display them so she had to double up. "I'm real and I believe we're cousins."

"I don't want to be rude, but I never knew I had a cousin until after my grandmother passed away."

Her eyes opened wide. "You never knew? Honestly?"

"No. Did you know about me?"

She snorted. "Of course I did. Our grandmothers were sisters, but they had a fight, I don't know what about. Hadn't spoken in years, but I knew of you."

"We moved to the States when I was little." I'd never had much family, so I wanted to be happy about finding this long-lost cousin. But Gran wasn't the sort of woman to cut people out of her life without a very good reason. I didn't know a lot about witches, but I knew there were bad witches as well as good ones.

I glanced into the corner to make sure Rosemary was busy, which she was, and lowered my voice. "Are you—" What was I doing? I couldn't ask a virtual stranger if she was a witch. I fumbled and asked if she was a Bartlett. Then I realized that her surname was Weeks.

She giggled and poked me in the arm with her index finger. "What you really want to know is am I a *witch*." She dropped her voice on the last word and imbued it with all the sinister drama she could manage, and it was quite a lot. In a normal voice she said, "Of course I am. Just like you."

How did this alarming young woman know that I was a witch before I did? I glanced at her ruby necklace, so much like my ring. I held up my hand. "Your necklace and my ring, they match."

"Our great-grandmother, the ancestor we share, broke up the set and gave one piece to each of her daughters. I have to be honest, I wore mine today so I'd know if you were my enemy or not."

Her necklace must have the same powers as my ring. And she was right, my ring wasn't glowing red and it wasn't hot. It was a relief to know this witch meant me no harm.

"I'm hoping we can be friends. In fact, I'm only in Oxford for the day; why don't I come back when you're closing, and we can go upstairs and you can tell me all about your life and I'll tell you all about mine. I'll even bring wine."

My mind was racing. Even though my ring wasn't setting off an alarm, her behavior was. All the while she was speaking to me her gaze was darting around the shop, as though she was looking for something. And she hadn't suggested we meet for a drink in a pub the way most new acquaintances would, she wanted to come upstairs to my home. Why? If my grandmother hadn't wanted me to know about the other side of my family, I needed to find out why.

I said, "I'd love to get together with you, but unfortunately I'm busy tonight. Give me your mobile number and I'll give you ring."

Annoyance flickered across her face like a cloud crossing the sun and she seemed much less friendly in that moment. But soon her expression cleared and, forcing a smile, she said, "Of course. Let's get together soon. And I can introduce you to my coven when you're ready." *Oh, goody.*

I put her number in my mobile and promised to call her. Before she left, I said, "Wait. You arranged Gran's burial."

"That's right. I tried to find your mother, but the university couldn't get hold of her. Your home in Massachusetts had voicemail. I left several messages."

"It's okay. I know we were hard to reach. I wondered where Gran is buried, that's all."

"Oh, in Moreton-under-Wychwood. You must come and visit. I'll take you there. Lots of our family are buried there."

I felt a flicker of pleasure when she said 'our family.' "I will."

"Don't be a stranger," she said, and then, "Blessed be."

The rest of the day passed uneventfully enough. We were busy. I enjoyed helping customers and listening to more stories about Gran. But I was definitely handicapped working in a knitting shop and not knowing how to knit. I was determined to learn. Surely someone in the vampire knitting club could teach me?

At the end of the day, I turned to ask Rosemary something and found her taking the cash out of the drawer. Due to the busy day, there was quite a bit of it. "What are you doing?"

"Just preparing the deposit," she said, with a casualness that sounded forced. "The bank's on my way home, no trouble at all." She looked almost desperate. Her eyes cut to the window where I saw the son with the pit bull tattoo staring in at us, his eyes squinted against the smoke from his rollup. When his gaze caught mine, my ring sparked heat, as though the tip of that cigarette had come close enough to scorch my finger.

"That's all right," I said. "I like to get a bit of a walk, anyway. I'll take the deposit. You go on home."

I thought she might cry, or argue with me, instead, her shoulders slumped and she nodded. "I'll see you Monday, then."

A woman with backbone would've told her not to bother coming in Monday, Tuesday or the Twelfth of Never. She'd been far too eager to get her hands on that cash, both she and her son made my ring hot, and my grandmother had already fired her once. But I couldn't do it. Not when she looked so downcast. I told myself that if I kept an eye on her and the cash, we'd muddle through.

She went out and met up with her son and as they walked up the street together, it looked to me as though they were arguing, again.

Rosemary was barely out of sight when there was a tapping on the door, which I had locked moments earlier and put up the Closed sign. I glanced out, surreptitiously. Sidney Lafontaine, the estate agent, stood there. I debated ignoring her, but she called out, "Hello Lucy. Your sweet little cat is so adorable posing in the window."

What could I do? I opened the door and tried to look firm. "I'm afraid we've just closed."

Clearly, I wasn't very good at firm. The woman brushed past me and said, "I won't stay a minute, but I brought the contract and the first payment." She set her attaché case on my cash desk as though she already owned the place, and pulled out a sheaf of documents and a bank draft. She smiled at me, a wide, white smile you see often in LA and almost never in England. "Richard Hatfield was very taken with you. His motto is, "Do business with people you like, and business will always be a pleasure."

"He should have that made into a bumper sticker," I said.

She chuckled as though I were the funniest comedian ever. "Here's the draft for one hundred thousand pounds. Just sign here." She pulled out a pen and flipped pages. There were several yellow stickers with arrows on them, all letting me know where to sign and initial. I'd never felt so railroaded. I could imagine elderly people being easily intimidated by these tactics. I was intimidated myself. And a hundred grand in Sterling isn't pocket change.

My jaw was aching and I realized my teeth were jammed together. I relaxed slowly and said, "I haven't made a decision about selling, yet."

"Oh, but all the others have signed. The deal will fall through without you."

"Why? Why can't Mr. Hatfield be happy with three lovely old shops? Why does he need four?"

She shrugged. "The rich have their whims. Take the

money, dear. You'll never get another offer as good."

"I haven't spoken to my mother, yet," I said, using my parent was the best excuse I had.

She chuckled again. I was going to have to start doing stand up if she was going to be in the audience. "We both know you're the owner now."

Wow, that was fast. "Still, I like to discuss everything important with my parents. But thanks for stopping by."

I went to the door and held it open. There wasn't much she could do, so she packed up her papers and that draft and, as she walked past me, said, "Don't leave it too long. I can't guarantee Richard won't move on to other projects."

I took the deposit to the bank and took a detour to walk off some of my frustration. I walked past groups of students heading out for the evening, past tourists, past couples heading into restaurants. I wished, quite suddenly, that I'd told my long-lost cousin I'd spend the evening with her. I was in one of the most beautiful cities in the world and I had no one to go to dinner with, or just hang out with. I didn't miss my old life, but I did miss my friends. If I was going to stay, I'd have make some new ones.

I picked up a takeaway curry for me and more tuna for Nyx and returned home. We both ate and then the kitten napped while I checked email.

My phone rang and it was my mother. Finally. "I've got bad news," I said, when we'd assured each other that we were fine and Dad was fine. "It's Gran." I told her Gran had died, sticking to the whitewashed version where heart trouble had taken her in her sleep. It was impossible to tell whether my mother believed the story since she was miles away and on a Sat phone.

The silence stretched. Was she crying? Then she said, "I'm sorry for you, Lucy. You were so close to her. Do you need me to come to Oxford?"

I hesitated. I didn't need her, and until we discovered who'd all but murdered Gran, I didn't want my mother in any danger. "There wasn't much to do. She was already buried when I got here." I asked if she knew about the other branch of our family and there was another pause.

"Yes, I knew, but we lived so far away, what was the point of telling you about relations you'd probably never meet?"

"I met my cousin today. She's the one who took charge of the burial since you and I were both unreachable."

"That was kind. What's she like?"

"She seemed nice." I didn't know how to describe Violet and we'd spoken so briefly I didn't know anything about her apart from the witch thing. I hadn't found out what she did, or what other family members there might be. "She lives in Moreton-under-Wychwood." At least I knew that.

"Ah, that's where Mother's people are from."

"I think she's buried there."

"In the family graveyard. Good."

"Did you know anything about Gran's will?" I finally asked.

"I know she planned to leave everything to you. Did

she?"

"Yes. But it seems wrong. You should have it."

My mother laughed. "What would I do with a knitting shop? I don't want to run it, and your father and I don't need the money. I'm happy for you to inherit, just don't let her force you into staying. You're a young woman with your life ahead of you. There's no obligation to continue Cardinal Woolsey's or step into your grandmother's shoes. Live your own life."

I'd wanted to talk Richard Hatfield's offer over with Mom, but I knew she'd advise me to sell. That's when I realized I had made up my mind. I wasn't selling. I wasn't going anywhere.

Sunday, I woke late, with the delicious feeling of a whole day off. All right, we'd only been open for two days, but it had been a very stressful two days. Deciding I needed some exercise, I changed into jogging clothes, divested myself of all my jewelry, tied back my hair and took myself for a run. I'm not big on jogging, but it's time efficient and sometimes, when things are bothering me, the simple act of pounding along pavement, struggling to breathe, actually helps calm me. I ran up to The Parks, with its twisting paths. No matter what time of the year, there's always something in bloom in the gardens and usually undergrads playing some kind of sport. There were plenty of joggers, most of whom passed me, dog walkers, lovers, and as I ran along the banks of the river, ducks, geese and swans. I perked up then. At least I was faster than the swans.

I clocked five km, decided that was plenty, and returned for a shower.

Amazingly, I did feel calmer when I got out of the shower. I changed into well-worn jeans and a sweatshirt, guiltily taking a break from the hand-knitted sweaters. I did some light housekeeping, giving Gran's room a good going over now I knew she wasn't so dead. I picked up a few groceries, chatted online with my friend Jennifer who never asked once when I was coming home.

Had she moved on already?

I hadn't finished the order the other night, due to unscheduled magic lessons. The shop was too busy when open for any administrative work, so I went back downstairs. Better to do it now when I could concentrate, even though this was my only day off in the week. Running a knitting shop was a lot more work than I'd imagined.

Nyx followed me, as usual. I was so used to my small, furry shadow, that I'd missed her on my run. When I got into the shop, I only turned on the lights behind the cash desk. I walked behind it, pulled out my order book and placed it on the counter and then something, I wasn't yet sure what, made me look up.

That was my only instinct. Something was wrong and I didn't know what. I felt a cool chill and glanced around. It wasn't a vampire in the vicinity this time. It was the front door to the shop that caught my attention.

It was ajar.

FIFTEEN

MY FIRST THOUGHT was irritation. I'd only had the lock changed a couple of days ago. Was the lock defective?

I headed toward it and at the same time I noticed splinters of wood suggesting the door had been forced open. I heard a soft footstep behind me. I started to turn when something hit me over the head. I cried out at the pain first and then felt my legs giving way beneath me.

* * *

Lucy! Lucy!" I heard a voice from a long way away. It was male and commanding and I didn't want to answer it, I wanted to sleep. "Wake up!" the voice said again. My eyes felt heavy and fought my efforts to lift them, but the voice was insistent and in the end it was easier to open my eyes than fight the force of his will.

"My head hurts," I said, as I opened my eyes. Rafe was bent over me, looking stern. I became aware that I was lying on the floor and struggled to sit up. He helped me and I found myself supported on his strong shoulders. "What happened?" I asked. I didn't like the feeble sound of my voice, which was trembling and didn't sound like my own.

"I don't know. Your cat came and got me."

I put a trembling hand to my head. It hurt, and I felt sick, and obviously my ears weren't working properly either. "Nyx came to get you? The trapdoor was closed and locked."

He squeezed my shoulder gently." Your cat is not a normal cat."

I couldn't think about that right now. The last moments of consciousness were coming back. "The door was ajar. Someone broke in and hit me over the head."

"Yes, you got quite the lump on the back of your head. You need to go to A&E."

I was furious. "What is so exciting about this little knitting shop that criminals equate it with the Bank of England?" I wanted to stand up but I was too dizzy. "And I can't go to hospital. I have work to do."

"No more today," he said gently.

He helped me to the visitor's chair and I sat, hoping the pounding in my head would ease soon. Rafe stayed by my side, as though he were afraid I would topple off the chair and onto the floor. Since I was afraid of this myself, I was quite happy to have him at my side, a protective presence. Also angry. I could feel his anger the way you feel heat coming off a radiator. "You could have been killed."

It was impossible not to think of Gran killed in this

very shop presumably under similar circumstances. "At least my attacker was wielding a club and not a knife." I had meant the words to come out jaunty and sarcastic but my voice trembled too much for that.

I was angry with myself for not being better prepared after what had happened to Gran. Well, I wouldn't make that mistake again. "Never mind changing the locks," I said. "I'm getting a proper security system in here."

"Excellent idea."

There was a rapping on the door and I jumped in my chair. Rafe made a sound like a growl and I saw the white gleam of his fangs, the first time I'd ever noticed them. Nyx stood on four stiff legs, her hair sticking out straight. Then a voice called out, "Lucy?"

I sighed with relief. "It's okay, it's the police."

Rafe seemed to center himself and the white gleam of fang was gone. He headed to the door and removed the umbrella he'd jammed under the knob to keep it closed. A uniformed police officer stood there and beside him was Ian Chisholm. The detective made one sweeping glance of my shop and then strode swiftly to my side. "Lucy, are you all right?"

I nodded, pleased to hear him sound so concerned.

"What happened?"

"I thought you didn't handle break-ins," I said with another weak attempt at sarcasm.

He and Rafe exchanged a glance, and I felt as though they were talking about me but I couldn't hear them. I felt ill and weak and frightened and the detective seemed so solid, and normal, a creature of the real world, the one I was most familiar with.

He and Rafe were Light and Dark, Living and Undead. I was in this bizarre state where I felt like I hovered between the two states.

Ian put a hand on my shoulder and said, "Hang on. An ambulance is on its way."

"But, I don't want an ambulance." I could have spared my breath; he was already heading to the back of the shop. I hoped Rafe had remembered to shut the trapdoor behind him when he came rushing to my side. I heard the cool, arrogant tone in which the vampire said, "I found her exactly like this."

"You haven't touched anything?"

"No."

The constable was standing outside, presumably waiting for the fingerprint guys to do my door handle. I was happy the cops were taking this break-in so seriously. I also wondered what was so special about the back room that both Rafe and Ian should still be in there. What could have been taken? The old mismatched chairs we used for knitting club? I got to my feet, feeling shaky but not bad enough that I'd faint. My legs were heavy and slow but I got to the curtain, which was pulled partly aside, and glanced in.

Oh, how I wished I hadn't. Rosemary was lying on the floor. She was on her back, her legs pulled up and to the side, like she was doing a yoga stretch. Her neck faced the other way from her knees and—I'm not sure how I knew—but I was certain her neck was broken.

Ian was squatting beside her. His hands were encased in blue latex gloves. Exactly the color of the Isle of Skye Mohair, which was a very peculiar thing to notice at that moment, but I suspect shock had something to do with it.

I think I made a sound. Of disbelief, pity, horror. Maybe I said actual words, I don't know.

Both men turned. "Lucy, sit down," they both said at the same moment.

Rafe took my arm and urged me back to the chair.

Ian followed and squatted in front of me, the way he had in front of the dead woman. His face was closed, professional. As though death was just part of the job, which I suppose it was. "That woman was your assistant, wasn't she?"

"Yes." My voice wavered. I cleared my throat and said, louder this time. "Yes. Her name was Rosemary Johnson."

"Did you expect her at work today?"

"No. The shop's closed on Sundays."

"Sir, I found this outside on the pavement." Another constable came in, holding a note in a plastic evidence bag. "It was blown against the side of the shop."

The paper was torn from a cheap scratch pad, handwritten in blue ink. She read the contents. "It says, 'I saw what you did. My silence will cost five thousand pounds. Meet me at the shop Saturday at midnight.'" She glanced up. "It's not signed."

"Good work," Ian said. "Get it to the lab."

He looked at me. "Does that note mean anything to

you?" He jerked his chin in the direction of the back room. "Could Rosemary have seen something that got her killed?"

I couldn't look at Rafe. Of course it meant something to me. *I saw what you did.* Had Rosemary seen whoever killed Gran and offered to keep quiet for five thousand quid? It was the only explanation I could find.

But Ian didn't know Gran had been murdered, so I said, "Could Rosemary have seen the person who broke into the shop the first time we had a break-in?"

He looked at me as though my bang on the head had scrambled my brains, which it probably had. "Five grand's a lot not to finger a thief. And most thieves don't turn to murder to cover their crimes."

It was a fair point. But a murderer covering their tracks with another murder? That sounded pretty plausible.

"Any idea what she was doing in the shop?"

"No. She left at five yesterday. She didn't even have a key to get back in." I must have looked as puzzled as I felt. "And why would she break in?"

"Perhaps she was killed elsewhere and carried to the shop," Rafe said.

"Why?" Ian asked him.

He only shrugged. I hated that we were withholding information from the police, especially information that could help solve Gran's murder. Even through my pounding head, I knew there was something I'd seen that was important. I rubbed my temples. Nyx jumped into my lap and licked my face with her sandpaper tongue, as though she could feel my distress. I pressed my face into her fur, and then it hit me. "Wait a minute," I said. "Can I see that note?"

Ian brought it over. I squinted at the words written in ordinary ballpoint pen. Then shook my head. "That's not Rosemary's handwriting. Her writing is much loopier, like a child's."

I tried to rise but simultaneously two hands came down my shoulders. Rafe on my left, and Ian on my right. I didn't have the strength to argue and, frankly, they were probably correct to keep me sitting. "I can show you a sample of her handwriting. It's in the order book." I looked at the counter where I'd been working. "Where's the order book?"

The constable glanced at the detective, and then back at me. "Order book, miss?"

"It's a big, leather bound book, about the size of photograph album. We write special orders and it and then, when we have enough, I put together one big order for the supplier. That's what I came down to work on. It was on the counter."

"There's nothing there."

"It must be there." I forced myself to standing and looked, but the desk was empty. The constable looked behind the desk and on the floor and shook her head.

"It's gone," I cried.

"What would someone want with your order book?" Ian asked.

But I was looking at Rafe. A big, old-looking

leather bound book. Was it possible that someone had mistaken the order book for the grimoire? And were they willing to kill for it?

* * *

"I don't need an ambulance," I insisted, even as the paramedics arrived to take me away.

Ian got right into my face. "You were knocked out completely and have no idea how long you were unconscious. It's entirely possible you have a concussion, or possibly worse. No arguments. We'll get you checked out and in the meantime we'll begin our investigation." The trouble with people asking you questions right after you regain consciousness is that you say things you later wish you hadn't.

"I just have a headache," I insisted.

He glanced at the broken door. "Is there someone you can stay with tonight? Until you can get that door fixed?" Better still, until they could find whoever had murdered Rosemary and bashed me over the head. I'd never felt so far away from home. "I don't know anyone in Oxford. I could probably stay next door but I don't want to worry the Miss Watts."

Rafe came closer. He'd obviously been listening to the conversation. "I can have the door made secure while Lucy's in the hospital. And I'll make sure someone keeps watch."

The two men looked at each other and it seemed that each stood to his full height. Ian asked, "And who might that be?"

Rafe said, "I'll do it myself." There was a strange energy between them, both antagonistic and, I thought, respectful, but I've never understood the way men communicate with each other. The face-off continued for a second and then the detective nodded.

* * *

That evening, I was sitting upstairs on the couch in what had been my grandmother's living room and I suppose was now mine. They had let me out of the hospital after running tests, all of which seemed to be fine. I had a headache, and a large lump at the back of my head, but no concussion and no serious damage. Except to my temper. I had just about had enough of this. First person-or-persons unknown had broken into the shop, then they had killed my poor grandmother, then my assistant, and they'd stolen my order book. Now they seemed to be after me. Why? Who could possibly benefit but another knitting shop owner?

The knitting shop business is not known for being cut throat.

Rafe had been waiting for me when I got back. I felt like a parcel being passed from one hand to another. The detective had been waiting when I was released from the hospital. He'd claimed he was there for another case, but I suspected that he wanted to drive me home for reasons of his own. However, I was too grateful for the ride to argue. I hadn't relished getting a taxi. To my relief, he hadn't questioned me anymore, just drove quietly as though he knew I didn't feel like making small talk after the events of the day.

When he dropped me off and I thanked him, he said, "I know you haven't been here long enough to make friends. But I'd like to be one of them. If you'll let me."

"Yes. I'd like that," I said, feeling grateful for his thoughtfulness.

The painkillers they'd given me had dulled the pain in my head to a throb. When I got back to the flat, Gran was with Rafe. She hugged me to her. I smelled the scent that always made me feel better. "You made gingersnaps!" I was so overwhelmed I nearly cried.

"I hate the idea of you in danger," she said.

I snagged a warm gingersnap and bit into it. Maybe it didn't help my aches and pains, but it reminded me I was loved and not alone. "I wish we could tell the police Gran was murdered"

"If you tell them, what's the first thing they're going to do?"

I sank to the couch. "Exhume the body."

Rafe spoke to me with infinite patience as though I was incredibly thick. "And if they exhume the body?"

"They won't find one." I said.

"Exactly. That's why we can't tell the police or anyone else that your grandmother was murdered."

"But that murder must be connected with Rosemary's. The note said, 'I saw what you did.' What else could she have seen but Gran's murder?"

197

"You said the note wasn't in Rosemary's writing," Rafe reminded me. "Maybe she was collateral damage?"

I'd been thinking about that in the hospital, where I'd had a lot of time to think, between tests. "I bet the note was written by her son."

"Randolph?" Gran asked. She shook her head. "He's not a nice young man."

"If he's on drugs, he'll do anything for money. What if Rosemary did see your killer and went home and told him?"

Gran's eyes widened. "I remember. She did come that day. My last day. She begged for her job back. She said she needed the money. She looked quite wild." Gran squeezed her eyes tight. "I told her I'd think about it." Her eyes were still shut and we both waited in case there was more. "Yes. I said I'd think about it. That son was the problem, I'm sure of it."

This fitted nicely with my theory. "Maybe she hung around, waiting for your answer. And she saw the murder. She went home and told her son what she'd seen and he decided to make a profit on the knowledge, penning a note supposedly from her."

"And the killer broke her neck to keep his identity secret."

SIXTEEN

I LOOKED AT Rafe. "Why did you suggest to Ian that Rosemary had been moved after she was killed?"

"I couldn't smell enough death. Besides, the way she was lying looked as though the body had been picked up under the shoulders and knees and put there, deliberately."

I shuddered. This wasn't like a cat bringing a dead mouse as a present, it was a cold-blooded murderer leaving a dead body in my shop for me to find. Why?

Rafe answered the question I hadn't asked. "Someone's trying to frighten you, Lucy."

"Well, it's working. And, again, why? And why didn't he kill me when I went down there?"

"I don't know."

He paced up and down. I might have paced too if my head didn't feel as though it might fall off my shoulders if I stood. "What did Dr. Weaver say when he examined Gran?" I asked Rafe. "Does he have any idea what kind of knife was used to stab her? Are we talking a butcher's knife? Stiletto? A steak knife?"

Gran had been following the conversation with an expression of increasing revulsion on her face. Finally, she said, "Would you like to see? The marks are still very fresh."

It hadn't occurred to me that, of course, I could examine her wounds myself. I didn't know much about the way vampires healed, but I guessed it wasn't the way people did. When I asked, Rafe said, "Vampires do heal much more quickly than humans, but your grandmother is still in transition. It will be a few more weeks before she's fully one of us."

This was excellent news. It had only been a few weeks since her attack so I hoped there would still be scars.

"We'll just go into the other room," she said to Rafe.

We went into the bathroom, and she bared her torso. As I looked at the damage someone had done to an elderly knitting shop owner, who also happened to be my grandmother, I was overcome with rage and a desire to hurt whoever had done this to her. There were two stab wounds. One in her belly and one in her chest. I thought she might have survived the one in her abdomen, but the one in her chest would have killed her. I wouldn't think it was an easy thing to stab someone in the chest. There are the ribs to get through, and one of the roles they play is to stop damage to vital organs beneath. Her killer had known what they were doing.

The scars were about an inch and a half wide, and there were round bruises at either side, as though two metal peas had pressed against her.

"Do these hurt you?" I asked.

She shook her head. "I don't feel much of anything, anymore. The one good thing is the aches and pains of old age are gone, too. I feel better than I ever did when I was alive."

"Well, that's good."

She looked at me with concern. "But I don't want you to be one of us. I want you to live your full and beautiful life and survive to be an old and crotchety lady."

"Gran, I want that too," I admitted.

"Then let's catch my killer."

I relayed my findings to Rafe.

He said, "We'll get the knitting club onto it."

"I beg your pardon?"

"We've got a dozen vampires with not enough to do, who can go out at night. They can eavesdrop on conversations, get talking to people in pubs late at night. Think of them as your Baker Street irregulars."

He was right. What an extraordinary gift it was to have a dozen vampires helping me solve this crime. Sherlock Holmes had his Baker Street irregulars, and I had my Harrington Street immortals. I felt certain that we would find Gran's killer, and whoever had stolen the order book. If Rafe and I were right, and it wasn't a rival knitting store wanting to steal our orders, then somewhere at this moment there was a very angry witch who, if she tried to cast a spell from that book, was going to end up knitting a jumper.

I had a pretty good idea who that witch might be and my blood began to boil.

"I do have a couple of tasks for the immortals," I said. "Find out where Rosemary's son, Randolph, is and get a sample of his handwriting. I'm sure he's the one who penned that note that got his mother killed. Maybe they can get him talking while he's high and find out who she saw that night. Who is Gran's killer?" I didn't care if she was family, if Violet or anyone connected with her had killed Gran, they would pay. By human law or otherwise.

"We'll find out everything he knows," Rafe promised. "What was the other thing?"

"Find out everything you can about Mr. and Mrs. Wright next door. Mr. Wright in particular. He showed me a dagger and I think it would make marks similar to those on Gran." I fetched a notepad and pencil. I'm no artist, but I managed to draw the dagger with the curved crosspiece ending in two metal balls.

"And now that you've given your orders, young lady, you can eat some dinner and go to bed," Gran said, quite sternly. I was only too happy to obey. She fed me soup and toast, and then a couple more gingersnaps before sending me off to my room. Nyx padded behind me and jumped on the bed. I was never so happy to have her company. I heard the low voices of Gran and Rafe in my lounge, and I knew they'd keep watch all night.

* * *

When I woke, Monday morning, Gran and Rafe were still there. Gran poured me a cup of coffee and while I drank it she said, "Rafe and I are agreed that you should close the shop today."

Naturally, I refused. I was made of sterner stuff. I'd had managed to survive heatstroke and sandstorms and various indignities when I'd gone to visit my parents on their archaeological digs. I thought I could manage one mostly-sleepless night and a headache.

And try not to think of a murderer who'd now killed two people connected with the wool shop.

I felt better after a shower, though the water touching my scalp made me wince.

A couple of painkillers helped, and, as I ate my breakfast, I asked Gran who could benefit from our family grimoire, since it seemed clear to me that whoever stole the order book had believed it was the spell book. She looked puzzled. "Most witch families have their own spell book. I suppose another witch might want ours, if there was a spell they particularly wanted, but it would be very unusual."

"Well somebody wanted it enough to kill two people for."

"Do you think that's what they wanted?" Gran asked.

"What else? The break-ins, the murders, what is so valuable in that knitting shop?"

Gran looked confused and sad. "Most witches are lovely women who celebrate female power and want to preserve the earth and help people. We aren't killers."

"Violet Weeks is part of our family, and she came to the shop Saturday. I swear she was looking around the whole time she talked to me and then tried to get me to invite her upstairs."

"You think she was after the grimoire?" Rafe asked.

"It's the only lead I've got." And it was a weak one, I had to admit. My ring hadn't even warmed when she was around. If she was a good enough witch, I suppose she could have deactivated it, or whatever the Wicca term would be for turning off my ruby ring's early warning system.

"But I don't understand," Gran said, looking bewildered. "If Violet Weeks stole the order book, thinking it was the grimoire, then who has the real grimoire?" Gran rubbed the heels of her hands against her eyes. "Oh, I wish I could remember things. I think I must have hidden it."

Rafe and I exchanged a glance.

"I don't remember why, but I was worried about the grimoire. Yes. I'm sure I tucked it away in a safe place."

My voice sounded hollow as I asked, "I don't suppose you remember where you hid it?"

She squeezed her eyes hard, concentrating, and finally opened them and even before she shook her head I knew she hadn't dredged up the memory of where she might have hidden the grimoire.

Someone knocked on the door connecting the shop to the flat. We all looked at each other and Rafe stood. I saw a flash of white at his mouth as he headed silently down the stairs. He returned a minute later with Sylvia and Alfred.

"Alfred paid a visit to Rosemary's son while you were sleeping."

It was great having detectives who worked while the rest of the world slept. "What did you find out?" I asked him eagerly. Alfred might not look like a heavy who'd get answers out of a guy with a pit pull tattooed onto his neck, but I suspected Alfred had hidden depths.

He shook his head. "Bad news, I'm afraid. Randolph Johnson overdosed. He was dead when I got there, a needle sticking out of his arm."

My first thought was, at least Rosemary was spared that pain. "Are you sure it was accidental?"

He shook his head. "Don't think it was. Looked to me like the kid was packing up to leave when somebody helped him to an overdose."

Rafe nodded. "Hoping the cops would think he killed his own mother, so high he didn't know what he was doing. Was she killed there, as well?"

Alfred's long nose seemed to quiver as though with scent memory. "Don't think so. Impossible to be certain. The smell of death was strong, but I think it was all from the boy."

Gran reached over and grabbed my hand. "Lucy, you can't go into work today, it's not safe."

I couldn't stand the thought of cowering in my home while Gran's, and now Rosemary's, murderer walked the streets. "I'm as safe there as anywhere. Customers come and go all day, and I only have to yell to have a dozen sleepy vampires come to my aid. Am I right?"

She didn't look convinced, but Rafe said, "She's right, Agnes. We'll keep an eye out." He turned to me. "I'll get Hester out of bed to act as your assistant until someone more suitable turns up."

"Hester? That surly teen?" I could think of few creatures I'd like less as my assistant.

"She's an excellent knitter, besides, she sleeps most of the night as well as the day and when she's awake she watches garbage on television or hangs about gaming." I had to smile. He sounded like an irritable parent. "She's got power, though. You'll be safe with her around."

I'd prefer to hire a new assistant myself, but I couldn't get one instantly. Rafe's solution gave me some protection, so I nodded. Sylvia walked forward and offered me a bag. "This should cheer you up."

Inside the bag, of course, was a sweater.

Sylvia had gone for glamour. The sweater she had knit was black and silver and looked like something created by an Art Deco designer. It featured intricate geometric patterns and when the light struck it the fabric shimmered. "This is too beautiful to wear in the shop." I said. "It's like something you'd see on a designer runway."

"I know," she said. "As an actress I learned early the importance of costume. You may feel fragile today, but wearing that sweater will fortify you. I promise." So she had been an actress. It made sense.

I slipped on the sweater and she was right. It did

cheer me up. I wore black trousers and a very simple black T-shirt so the sweater had no competition. I added big silver earrings and, once more, the silver chain with the cross that I had purchased from the antique dealer. Sylvia surveyed me critically. "Red lipstick, my dear. You're pale and have dark shadows under your eyes, the red lipstick will draw the eye to your mouth."

"No one will have eyes for anything but this beautiful sweater," I said. But I went to my meager cosmetic supplies and found a red lipstick that I'd bought one Christmas. I felt a bit overdressed for a knitting shop, but everything in my life and been so extraordinary since I'd arrived here that looking like a glamorous 1920s movie star seemed perfectly ordinary.

The police had quickly determined, as Rafe had suggested, that Rosemary hadn't been killed in my shop, which meant the crime scene people were gone within hours. It still gave me a very strange feeling to walk into that shop, knowing Rosemary wouldn't be coming in today, or any day. I had to keep blinking away the image of her lying in the back room like a broken doll.

Maybe I hadn't liked her much, but she had done a good job when I'd reopened the shop and I wanted to avenge her death as well as Gran's.

Fortunately, since I wasn't exactly on top form, and my assistant was both undead and uncooperative, Monday was a quiet day. Hester yawned in an exaggerated fashion every time I asked her to do anything and moped around wearing all black, though her jumper at least was hand-knitted. Fortunately, the initial rush to visit Cardinal Woolsey's and express condolences or stock up, in case the place shut, had passed.

Nothing dramatic happened, for which I was grateful except that, like the days before, my sweater aroused so much interest that, as Sylvia had predicted, we sold all the silver and most of the black wool. Once more, it was impossible to find the pattern, since she had invented it, but I managed to find two or three patterns that could be adapted.

When there was a lull, Hester got out her cell phone, stuck earbuds in her ears and zoned out. "Hester, if we don't have customers, look busy. Tidy the patterns, sweep the floor."

She stared at me sullenly. "Or what? You'll dock my pay?"

I may not have had four centuries of practice being a hard ass, but in my twenty-seven I've learned a thing or two. I stared her down and said, "Or I'll tell Rafe and let him deal with you."

"Ooh, I'm so scared," she said, opening her brown eyes wide, but she took her earbuds out and smartened up after that. I let her go at four so she could 'grab a nap' before heading out on whatever wild adventures she had planned that night.

At the end of the day, when I'd taken the deposit to the bank and returned, fatigue and the remains of the headache caught up with me.

I'd arranged to have the locksmiths arrive after five, which involved a lot of grumbling and a large premium.

I also asked for a price on an alarm system with security cameras.

As soon as the new lock was in, I secured the door behind me, went upstairs and fell into a deep and dreamless sleep.

I woke up, had some dinner and more painkillers and then I began to search for the grimoire. If witches were willing to kill for it, then I was determined to find the thing and, possibly, destroy it. Gran hadn't been able to remember where she'd hidden the spell book, but common sense suggested it was in the house somewhere, especially as she'd asked Rafe to look after it for her when he returned from America. She'd been killed before he returned, but the book must be close.

I wanted to use my witch powers to help find the grimoire, but I had no idea how to access them. I went with the tried and true human method of finding lost items. I turned out cupboards, looked behind furniture, took every single book out of every bookcase. Nyx had a wonderful time, poking her head into open drawers, exploring behind the furniture, and generally making the job more playful. We found nothing.

Smut covered and dusty, I collapsed on the floor and played with Nyx before tackling the last possible hiding place.

The attic.

The attic in my gran's house in Oxford was nothing like the one in our house in the States. It involved pulling a ring in the ceiling of Gran's bedroom, then yanking down a ladder, and finally climbing up the ladder into a space too small to stand up in except at the very middle. There was some old junk up there, a few boxes, and three old steamer trunks. I knew I wouldn't rest until I'd turned them out, so I began systematically checking what was up here.

I began with the first steamer trunk, tossing billows of dust in the air as I opened the lid. The dust should have told me it hadn't been opened in decades, but with magic in the house, who knew how Gran might have magicked the hiding place.

Inside the trunk were albums and boxes of photos. I opened the album on top. There was Gran and my grandfather getting married, and Mom as a baby, toddler and young child. Then many fewer photos taken in this house.

I flipped to the end of the album. There was Gran celebrating Cardinal Woolsey's fiftieth year in business.

I put that aside to take back downstairs with me. Digging deeper I discovered a box of loose photos that showed Gran as a child. They were all black and white, but quite clear. Sure enough, a dark-haired girl a bit older than Gran shared most of the pictures with her. Was this my great-aunt? The one I'd never heard of until recently?

I'd be here all night if I looked at every picture, so I resolved to take one box of photos down with me, and that album, and return at regular intervals to sort through the rest. There was no grimoire in this trunk, however, so I moved on to the next.

The second trunk smelled of lavender and moth

balls. Inside was an old wedding gown, all packaged in tissue. Assorted clothes, some baby toys, old magazines and knitting patterns. Again, no grimoire.

I got to the third trunk and more junk met my eyes. I was beginning to feel that this was a hopeless task. I took everything out, wondering who would save a broken pair of opera glasses, handbags from half a century ago, old gloves and bits of fabric.

The last item was a mirror. A big oval hand mirror with interesting writing and symbols decorating the edges. I'd have to get my parents to interpret those for me. The glass was wavy with age but when I looked in the mirror I thought it reflected back a softer version of myself, something like the mirrors they use at cosmetics counters to encourage you to buy more. I was surrounded by the contents of all three steamer trunks and there wasn't a book to be seen.

"Grimoire, where are you?" I wailed aloud up there all alone in the attic. I caught movement out of the corner of my eye and noticed that my reflection was breaking up in the mirror. It was like a still lake when you throw a stone in it, and as my image receded, another emerged to take its place.

I could feel my eyes widening as I looked. I saw a very ordinary bookshelf absolutely crammed with books. And, on the top, pushed there as though the person who owned the bookcase had discovered one more volume and had no more space, was an old volume, with a cracked leather spine. With a shiver of recognition, I knew I was looking at the missing grimoire.

Even as I tried to take a mental picture of the bookcase, looking for any clues as to where it might be, exactly, the image faded away and my own, very puzzled face, once again stared back at me.

I didn't know exactly where it was, but I knew the grimoire wasn't in Gran's house or shop.

I'd recognized the setting, though. Wherever that spellbook was, I had been there. If only I could think more clearly.

I headed back down the ladder, clutching the mirror in one hand, the photo album and box of loose photos clamped between elbow and ribs. I'd have to return for the rest.

* * *

I decided to run downstairs to the vampires' nest. Nyx was at my side, my magic mirror clutched in my hand. I'd resisted asking it who was the fairest of them all, but only just.

I opened the door that separated the flat from the shop and nearly had a heart attack. A scary looking man was standing there. In a nanosecond I recognized Rafe and sagged with relief. "What are you doing here?"

"Coming to see you."

"Oh, I was coming to see you. Well, all of you." I showed him the mirror. "It's magic," I said, my eyes round. "I saw the grimoire."

"A scrying mirror. Excellent. I'll take you back

then, so you can show your grandmother. And next time, call me and I'll escort you. Now, especially, with this maniac on the loose, you're not to be left alone."

It was certainly nice having someone so big and strong and dangerous accompany me to the vampire lair. He opened the door and called out, "Lucy's here," presumably so they could all make themselves decent. Whatever that meant to a vampire.

As I walked in I heard a snarling noise and saw Hester sitting in a large, wooden chair that I didn't remember seeing before. Her fangs glittered and she glared at me. "What's wrong, Hester?" She hadn't been growling and fanging me when she'd left the shop.

"Hester is grounded," Rafe answered coolly. "She was ordered to stay with you until the shop closed and she disobeyed."

"Grounded?" I wanted to laugh, but Hester looked as though she'd have my liver for breakfast at the first giggle.

I wanted to make things easier for her, so I said, "But if she's grounded, how will she help in the shop tomorrow? I need her."

Hester looked at me with less hatred and more respect as Rafe considered the matter. I doubted he'd ever had kids, but Gran had, and she looked at the scenario playing out and said, "Perhaps if Hester apologized to Lucy, and promises not to let her down again, she could still go out tonight."

I wanted Hester's apology like I wanted bunions, but I knew Gran was trying to let them both save face.

Rafe looked down his long nose at both of them and said, "Fine."

Hester said, "Sorry," in a sulky tone. Before Rafe could snap at her, Gran said gently, "And you won't let her down again."

"I won't."

"Very well." They both looked at Rafe who nodded abruptly. Hester jumped from the chair and ran through the doorway, calling, "I'm late. Come on. Who pinched my black eyeliner?"

SEVENTEEN

"LUCY," GRAN SAID, looking pleased to see me. She was paler than before but more solid. She seemed less human and more vampire every time I saw her. She still looked her age, but sleeker and stronger. "Did you find the grimoire?"

"No, I found this, instead." I held up the mirror. "It showed me the grimoire, but then the picture faded. Shouldn't the mirror lead me to what I seek?"

Sylvia sent me the sort of look she usually reserved for Hester. "It's a scrying mirror, Lucy, not Google Maps."

"Well, it showed the book, I'm sure it was the right one, in a jumble of other books. Does that ring any bells?"

Gran looked distressed, and said, "Let me see. Perhaps I can try the scrying mirror. I handed it to her and she held it up, then her lips made an O. I went behind her to see what she was seeing but there was nothing there but a corner of my own face. Belatedly, I realized vampires have no reflection, so magic mirrors weren't in their bag of tricks.

I began to pace. Rafe joined me. I said to him, "She never gave you any idea where she was going to hide the grimoire?"

"No. She planned to give it to me for safekeeping, but she was killed before she could. I thought the killer must have got away with the book."

"But, if whoever attacked me thought that the order book was the grimoire, then they didn't get it."

"There is another possibility," he said. I had a sense that I wasn't going to like his second possibility but I asked anyway. "What is it?"

"There's more than one individual, or group, who wants that book."

I felt as though cold, clammy hands were gripping my upper arms. "Who would want a book of spells other than a witch? Or someone training to be a witch?"

Rafe wasn't given to quick answers. He pondered my question. "The grimoire itself has value as in antiquity, and a piece of art. I suppose there are collectors who might go to great lengths to get their hands on such a book, but would they kill for it?"

"I hope not. It's bad enough feeling that maniacal witches are after me, I'm not sure I can take murderous bibliophiles as well."

"Based on that bump on the back of your head, I don't think this is a laughing matter."

He was right, of course. I'd been lucky to escape with only a bump when Gran had fared so much worse. If Nyx hadn't brought Rafe to me so fast, I wondered if I'd still be alive.

"Let's suppose that Gran knew someone, or something, was closing in. You were away and she was worried that it would fall into the wrong hands. Where would she hide it?"

"Not here. We searched every inch of the shop and your home."

"And I don't think we're the only ones who have searched. I bet Gran asked you to take the book after that first break-in. So, if we assume that whoever attacked me didn't get what they were looking for, then it's still well hidden."

"Not on the premises, but close by, because we know she had planned to put it in my hands for safekeeping."

I snapped my fingers, loud in the thick silence of our joint pondering. I turned to him, "Where would you hide an antique so it wouldn't stand out?"

He looked at me and his brows drew together before he nodded, slowly. He didn't speak, so I did, even though I was fairly certain he knew where I was going with this. "You might hide it in an antique store that is so jumbled no one can ever find anything."

"But would she be so foolish? Anyone could go into the antique store and buy the grimoire."

"They'd have to know it was there, and find it, and, in that jumble, it would be a miracle."

It was after midnight by this time. The vamps were obviously anxious to get on with their plans, so I got up to leave. I'd go to Pennyfarthing's the next day during shop opening hours while Hester manned the shop and and have a good look through the books.

I was nearly at the door when Sylvia said, "Oh, Lucy, Dr. Weaver left you this package."

Dr. Weaver had style. The lumpy package Sylvia passed me was wrapped in pink tissue paper, tied with silver ribbon, and bore a card. In careful handwriting, Dr. Weaver had written, "May this brighten your day and speed your healing." I tore into the wrapping and discovered a cardigan hand-knit by the doctor. It was purple and pink, and decorated with overblown roses. I couldn't help but feel happy when I saw it.

Once again Rafe walked me home. When we got to my door, he said, "Where does it hurt?"

I pointed to the lump on the back of my head. He reached out and ran his palm over the spot, his touch as soft as a whisper, then he continued to move his hand down my neck and over the top of my back. The sensation was like cool water running over me. Not unpleasant at all. In fact, I felt the remaining headache lift. He left his hand on my back a moment longer than necessary and I looked into his dark, mysterious eyes. With a slight smile, he leaned in and kissed my cheek. "Good night, Lucy."

I put my hand to the spot where he'd kissed me. As he walked away I echoed, softly, "Good night."

* * *

Hester not only turned up the next morning, but she arrived on time. She was even marginally more useful. Sylvia, or maybe Clara, must have suggested the outfit she wore for it was much more in line with what a knitting shop assistant should wear. A longish black skirt over short boots, and on top was a beautiful cardigan in green and black with big silver buttons.

Not wishing to rush into Pennyfarthing the moment it opened, and be conspicuous as the first customer, I waited a couple of hours and around eleven that morning went next door.

When I got there I was aware of voices. There must be other customers, which was good for me, as I wanted to browse and poke around without anyone paying attention to me. Bookcases were scattered randomly all over the shop and so crammed with titles that, if given a choice, I'd have preferred to search for the proverbial needle in the haystack.

However, there were no other customers in the shop. Mrs. Wright was standing at the sales counter at the top of the shop and with her was her husband. They stopped talking when they saw me. She looked as though she'd been crying. The American in me wanted to ask her if everything was all right, but my British side urged restraint. Since I was on British soil I chose to pretend I saw nothing amiss when she asked, in a choked voice, if she could help me.

"I wondered if you had any knitting books."

Mrs. Wright plucked a tissue from a box on the counter and surreptitiously wiped her eyes while pretending to blow her nose. Perhaps to give her time, her husband said, "Knitting books? You run a knitting shop. Don't you sell knitting books?"

I hadn't expected a third-degree interrogation as my excuse was, admittedly, flimsy. I said, "We do. We sell modern ones, but there's a particular series that my grandmother said was very good if you're learning to knit. It's out of print. I'm probably on a wild goose chase, but,I thought, since you're right next door, that I might have a look."

My hand felt suddenly hot and when I looked down I saw that my ring was glowing. I thought of the way Mr. Wright had nearly stabbed me with a Prussian sword and wondered if he was as doddery as he seemed. But why would he want to hurt Gran?

By this time, Mrs. Wright had her emotions under control. She said, "I'm not sure if we have any knitting books, but they'd be on one of the shelves over there." She waved a hand in the general direction of the middle of the shop. I got the feeling this was pretty much how she directed every customer to every item they were searching for. Basically, you were on your own.

The warmth on my ring finger made me want to run, but how dangerous could it be with the shop open to customers and my vampire protectors right next door?

I decided to keep an eye on Mr. Wright, but go clockwise and systematically search bookshelves. I'd begin at the top, like the vision I'd glimpsed in the mirror, but what if the mirror was faulty? Or a trickster? I'd look at every book on every shelf before I gave up.

I didn't go straight to the glass-fronted bookcase that held the oldest books, because that would have been too obvious. I thought, if my grandmother had hidden the grimoire here, she'd slipped it into an obscure spot.

Ancient and dusty textbooks on everything from

astronomy to zoology bumped spines with well-read Enid Blytons and mass-produced copies of Dickens, Trollope, and Austen. To my surprise, I did find a good knitting primer from the 1950s. The pictures and patterns alone made it quite a good conversation piece and I decided to buy it to display in the shop.

While I was mooching through old cookbooks, stacks of ancient Vogue magazines and a book of ancient Greek plays, Peter Wright spoke, from behind me, "What about this one?" The Wright's son held out a book of crochet patterns from the 1970s. "I heard you from the back room." He pointed to the cover that featured a bedspread made of colored squares. "Remember the Granny Square? I think Mum covered everything in our house in those things."

"Thanks," I said, stacking the crochet book on top of the knitting book. He said he'd take them to the till for me and I could keep looking.

However, after hunting through the rest of the bookcases I had no more to show for my search than that one knitting book, one crochet book and an incipient dust allergy. Mr. Wright rang them up. I said, as casually as I could, "What happened to those swords and the dagger you were polishing last time I was in? Did you sell them?"

He peered at me as though from a long distance away, and then said, "No. We keep them locked up. Did you want to see them?"

When I assured him I didn't, he said. "That will be seven pounds seventy-five, then, please."

As I left, Mrs. Wright was standing near the door staring out into the street. She still looked very troubled. I said, unable to hold off the American side of me any longer, "Is everything all right Mrs. Wright?"

She seemed startled by the question. Her eyes, still red from crying, blinked at me a few times and then she said, "Oh yes. Only it's so difficult, isn't it?"

I had no idea what was so difficult, but I nodded in an understanding fashion, put my books under my arm and headed back. I peeked in the window and could see there were no customers and I didn't feel up to making small talk with my surly assistant.

I was bitterly disappointed that I hadn't found the grimoire. I'd been so sure I'd find it next door.

I texted Hester that I had a few more errands to run and headed into Elderflower Tea Shop. My grandmother always used to say problems were best solved over a cup of tea. Add a scone slathered with jam and cream, and I'm inclined to agree with her. Both Miss Watts were working today and it was quiet in the tea shop. They seemed delighted to see me. They both came over. "Are you all right? We were so shocked. Poor Rosemary."

Of course, they'd heard about the murder. I imagined that soon the press would get hold of the story and everyone would know. Still, lovely British ladies that they were, they didn't pry, but gave me one of the best tables by the window and I settled in with my pot of tea, my scone, and my knitting book.

Reading that knitting book was like travelling back

in time. Cheerful housewives knitted sweaters for all the family as well as dresses, coats, blankets and scarves.

As I was contemplating the need for a tea cozy shaped like a fruit basket, overflowing with knitted fruit, I became aware of a strange sensation at the back of my neck. It was like raindrops, only not wet, like cold fingers drumming on the back of my neck without any pressure. In short, it was a strange and peculiar sensation almost impossible to describe.

I glanced up and looked around. Outside the window Nyx sat on the other side of the road staring up at me. You wouldn't think, considering that I was across the street and behind a window, that I could see her eyes, but I swear I could, green and glowing strangely. I blinked, wondering if I was coming down with something, and Nyx narrowed her eyes, I swear she did, as though irritated with me.

What on earth did she want? I'd go downstairs and fetch her, I thought, now that I'd finished my tea. Maybe Hester was refusing to let her into the shop. It wouldn't surprise me.

I went to the front to pay my bill but the two cups of tea had had their effect. After settling my bill, I said, "I'll pop to the loo and be on my way." This is what happens when you spend too much time in Oxford, you say things like, "I'll just pop to the loo." The toilet was up a flight of stairs and as I rose higher the strange dripping, drumming feeling at the back of my neck increased. Did I have some remaining trauma from being hit over the head?

At the top of the stairs was a discreet sign pointing me to the facilities. The bathroom was to the left down the corridor, and the one that led to the private apartments of the Miss Watts was to the right. The tingling increased as I turned and recognized the bookcase in the hallway leading to the sisters' flat.

I had seen that bookcase in the scrying mirror.

Of course, that's why the location had looked familiar. I'd been here before but never paid any attention to the bookcases. Glancing quickly behind me to make sure no one else was coming up the stairs, I ducked down the private hallway. Those bookcases had been there as long as I could remember, and, since I didn't think the Miss Watts were great readers, I doubted the books had been disturbed in some time.

I began rapidly to scan shelves but there were so many books. Old paperbacks, coffee table books from fifty years ago, novels, travel guides to every spot in England. I pulled out a driving guide to the Lake District from the 1940s and nearly cried when I saw that behind it was another row of books. They'd run out of room and simply shelved books in front of other books.

I drew in a deep breath, closed my eyes and pulled up the vision exactly as I had seen it in the scrying mirror. The book I was looking for had been pushed on top of the bookcase. I couldn't see it from here but I felt it was there, above me and out of sight.

I needed to step on something to make me taller but there was no handy chair or stepstool. I reached my hands up as high as I could, straining on tiptoe but couldn't quite get to the top of the shelves. Hoping no one would need the facilities anytime soon, I grabbed oversized books off the bottom shelf. Kings and queens of England, country walks in Oxfordshire, a history of Trinity College, and a driving guide to Sussex were all sturdy looking.

These coffee table books hadn't sat on a coffee table in many years, based on the dust covering them. I stacked the books and then gingerly stepped on my rudimentary footstool. This give me just enough height to reach up and feel along the top of the shelves. I came across an old cardboard box, something spiky that felt like a huge shell, enough cobwebs to furnish a haunted house, and finally, by reaching so far sideways I nearly fell off my stack of books, I touched leather. Old, dry leather that was clearly the spine of a book.

By this time, the feeling on the back of my neck was pronounced. I couldn't grasp the book, so, in frustration, I climbed down, moved the stack of books a foot to the right and climbed back up. This time, I was able to reach the book with both hands. I took it down, my heart hammering, and the back of my neck feeling as though the cast of Riverdance were doing a particularly energetic number on my nape.

The book was clearly old, but if I had expected it to be covered with mysterious symbols, I was sadly disappointed. On the surface, it looked no more interesting than any old leather bound book. Was this even the grimoire? If the tingling on the back of my neck was anything to go by, then it was.

With another quick glance to make sure I was alone, I tried to open the book. It didn't open.

I tried again, gently using my thumbs to pry open the book's cover. Again, nothing happened. Gran's protection spell was working, then.

From down below I heard Miss Watt say, "Oh yes, just at the top of the stairs at the end of the corridor and turn left."

Rapidly, I slipped the book that wouldn't open into the bag along with my knitting and crochet books. Then I knelt down and quickly shoved the coffee table books back approximately where they had been. I rounded the top of the banister and began down the stairs just as an old man wearing a stained raincoat and walking with a cane began to ascend. There wasn't room for two of us on the stairway so I backed up.

He gave me a curious look as he passed me with a murmured thanks and I wondered if he could somehow sense my agitation.

I scampered down the stairs and slipped out the front door so I wouldn't have to see the Watt sisters. I knew it was ridiculous, but I felt like a thief even though I was almost certain this was, in fact, my own property. If I was wrong, I would return the book, but I didn't want to face them feeling so jumpy. Nyx joined me as I left the tea shop, her tail twitching as we walked back to Cardinal Woolsey's. I had the oddest feeling she was protecting me.

When I got back to the shop, Hester was helping a woman who'd seen a crochet pattern for a cushion in a magazine. She couldn't remember the name of the magazine, its date or anything but that she thought the cushion had wavy, colored lines on it and was pretty.

Hester led her to where we kept patterns and seemed perfectly able to handle the order, so I gave her a wave to let her know I was back, and then carried the precious grimoire upstairs to my flat.

Where could I hide it? Even though I knew I'd be downstairs for the rest of the day, the way strange things had been happening around here, I didn't want to take any chances. If I could find the spell book with a scrying mirror, perhaps any witch could.

I'd read over the years various ways to keep things safe, putting them in places where thieves would never look. I couldn't imagine putting this beautiful old book in a laundry basket or a garbage can. After wandering around for a couple of minutes, I put the book inside my suitcase in the back of the cupboard in my room. Then I stacked the extra quilts and pillows and blankets that Gran kept in my room over top of it, hoping it looked as though it were an old suitcase that no one ever used.

I went back downstairs, very careful to make sure the door was once more locked. No one could get up there without passing me and I was going to be very careful not to turn my back on any customers, no matter how innocent they looked. I glanced at my assistant and it seemed to me that she wore a shifty, guilty look. I wouldn't turn my back on her, either.

It was four clock. Another full hour before I could close.

It was the longest hour of my life.

Hester kept yawning, which didn't help. Finally, at a quarter to five I told her to go. She glared at me and reminded me that yesterday I'd let her go early and Rafe had put her in the naughty chair.

"If Rafe questions you, tell him I'm closing early."

She looked as though this might be a trick to get her grounded again.

"I really am. If Rafe gives you any trouble, send him to me." No one's life would be ruined if I closed ten minutes early. Knitting is not a craft fraught with emergencies, and I was dying to get upstairs and have another look at that grimoire.

Once she'd left, I was about to close when the doorbell jingled its merry tune. Grrr. I hoped this customer would be quick. I put on my *how can I help you* face and turned to see Peter Wright standing inside the door.

"Peter," I said, feigning calmness even as the ring on my hand began to burn. "I was about to close up."

He smiled, and for the first time I noticed how creepy his smile was. "Good. I want to talk to you, privately." Before I could answer, he'd locked the door and flipped my open sign to closed.

"How can I help you?" I didn't understand why he was a danger, but, not only my ring, but every sense in my body, both human and witch, clanged an SOS. From the corner of my eye I saw Nyx stand in her basket, her back arched and her mouth open in a silent hiss.

EIGHTEEN

HE WAS CARRYING a leather satchel and reached into it. I flinched but nothing more deadly emerged than paper. He said, "We really need you to sign this agreement so we can sell the shops to Richard Hatfield."

"We? You don't own the shop next door, your parents do."

"Yeah, well, they're old and I need that money. I've gotta get my kids back. My wife won't let me see them. She says I'm not a proper influence."

Imagine.

He began breathing hard as though thinking about his ex made him crazy. "I need a good lawyer and a stable home. Those things cost money."

"Peter, I feel for you, I really do, but I promised Gran I'd run the shop. I'm sorry, but I'm not selling."

"Let me make this simple for you," he said, pulling something else out of the bag. It was the dagger. I could hear his father now, showing it off to me. *It's a double-bladed dagger from the sixteenth century, I reckon. Lovely piece. Look at the way the cross-guard curves.*

The loops at the end would make bruises the size of peas when the dagger was pushed into a person's body.

"You killed my grandmother." I had trouble getting the words out around the anger burning in my chest. "For money?"

"I wouldn't have, if she'd been reasonable. And I won't kill you, either, if you're reasonable. I worked out that once she was gone, you lot in America would want to get rid of the place. That's what you should do. Sell up and go home."

His words buzzed around me like so many flies around dung. But I was thinking, seeing things in a new light. "Rosemary. She saw you kill Gran, didn't she?"

As we were talking, he was urging me back, into the back room where I'd found Rosemary. Since I was at the pointy end of a very sharp dagger, I went. He held up his free hand. "Hey, that's not on me. That old cow and her son tried to blackmail me."

That blackmail note hadn't made sense until now. The meeting was set for 'the shop' at midnight and I'd assumed it was this shop. But Rosemary hadn't been killed here. "She met you in Pennyfarthing, thinking you'd pay up."

"I wasn't going to pay her, when I hadn't got the money from the shop sale yet. How could I? When she saw me getting agitated, she said if she didn't get home in an hour, her son would call the police." He shrugged, as though his subsequent actions were entirely reasonable. "What could I do? It was their own fault. Greedy sods."

And he, of course, wasn't one.

I had to do something, but all I could think of was to keep him talking. Maybe Rafe would come looking for me. I didn't think I had long, though. I've heard the term blood lust. Now, looking into Peter's eyes, I saw it. He wanted to kill me. Whatever I did, he was going to stab me to death and enjoy himself. His eyes looked drugged on the excitement.

Still, as a plan to get money together to get his kids back, I didn't think this one was entirely sound. "And what happens if I don't sign that agreement and you kill me?"

"Sidney Lafontaine did some research. You inherited from your grandmother, but if you die, then everything goes to your mother. We all know she doesn't want a knitting shop. She'll sell it."

"Unless I have a will. Which I do. I've left everything to a cat shelter. By the time the charity's board of directors make a decision? Your kids will be adults." I had no idea if I was talking garbage, but I had to keep him talking and not stabbing.

He looked momentarily taken aback. Good. Then he scoffed. "No, you haven't. Come on, I don't have time to waste." He pushed the contract at me, holding the dagger near my throat.

"Do you have a pen?" I asked. This was ridiculous. Though, somehow, a deadly dagger held by an ex-military guy isn't ridiculous. I should have realized, when I saw the expert way he'd stabbed through Gran's ribs that the killer had training. How stupid I'd been.

"Bloody hell." He dug in his pocket, felt in his satchel.

Keep him talking. "Why did you put Rosemary's body here and then hit me over the head?"

"I put her body in here because I wanted to frighten you away. I wouldn't have knocked you out, but you came down to the shop when you had no business being there." He looked at me like I was stupid. "You close on Sundays."

"If I'd known you were down here, believe me, I'd have stayed away."

"I heard you coming, and I couldn't let you see me." He shrugged like bashing me over the head was perfectly reasonable behavior.

I had powers. There must be something I could do. I recalled making the wools float around. At least I could do that. My fingertips were tingling at the thought. Not that I'd get far bopping him on the head with balls of floating wool. Why hadn't Gran opened a rock and fossil shop?

The vampire deterrent basket was still in the corner, beside the broom. In it were sharpened wooden knitting needles, more useful against tiny vampires than a human maniac, I suspected. There was also a crucifix and the jar of holy water.

He was rummaging in the satchel with the hand holding the contract, his other hand holding the dagger against my throat. I tried to forget the knife and focus. I pictured the jar of holy water and willed it to rise and come toward me. I felt my power, like warmth rushing through me, and, behind his shoulder, *yes*, I saw the jar begin to rise. "Strike this murderous devil," I said aloud, "Holy water douse this evil."

"What?" he said, and then he turned to look and yelled as the jar flew at him, hitting him in the forehead with such force that the jar broke and the water gushed into his eyes blinding him.

I pushed him away and tried to run, but he grabbed my arm. He hadn't dropped the knife. I knew I only had a second before he regained his sight. Frantically, I tried to pull away.

Nyx hissed and jumped onto his face, clawing and scratching. He screamed, flailing with his knife hand, trying to stab her. My fury grew and I punched the arm holding the knife, but he held it in a vice grip. "Broom," I yelled, "Sweep away this dirt." Then, "Knitting needles, fill my empty hands." I made the finger-waving gestures to go with my shouted commands. I had no idea where the words were coming from, but I followed instinct.

The broom flew up. It was a heavy whisk broom with a wooden handle, no doubt the kind witches fly on. As it obeyed my command, it turned and jammed Peter Wright in the belly, about where he'd stabbed Gran.

An old broom may not look like much when it's leaning in the corner with dust and cobwebs clinging to its straw, but get it going fast enough, and the hardwood handle can do some damage. He grunted in pain and doubled over. The broom struck again, and again. Meanwhile, the sharpened needles flew into my hands and I stabbed my attacker in the wrist until, at last, he dropped the knife.

While I grabbed the knife and jumped back, Nyx hissed and attacked his face yet again. He dashed a hand across his eyes where the holy water still seemed to blind him.

Nyx had scratched his face, the jar had wounded his forehead and the broom was still whacking him. "Stop," he yelled. "Make it stop."

At that moment the trap door flew open and Rafe appeared, fangs bared, ready for vengeance.

There was also banging on the front door, and a shout of, "Armed police, stay where you are." And I heard the front door being bashed in.

Again.

A team of cops ran in, all with their guns drawn. Ian was right behind them, his grim look easing when he saw I was unhurt.

I dropped the knife, not because I thought anyone would think I was the perp and shoot me, but because I was done. I trembled all over and sat down on one of the chairs before my legs buckled.

"Hold on," Rafe said in my ear, putting an arm around me. "You're all right."

Peter was handcuffed and being read his rights. I looked at Ian and raised my brows. "Five minutes earlier would have been good."

"Do you need an ambulance?"

I followed his glance and found my hand was bleeding. Must have happened when I grabbed for the knife. I shook my head. "Just a knick."

"How did *you* know Lucy was under attack?" Rafe asked. He sounded angry, but I knew it was because Ian had almost arrived before he did. And both of them were nearly too late.

"Rosemary Johnson's son died of a suspicious overdose. Peter Wright's prints were found at the scene. I went to interview him and his parents said he'd popped over here. Then his mum burst into tears and said he'd taken an old dagger. That's when I called the Armed Response Unit."

I nodded. "He needed money, you see. There's a developer who wants this whole block of shops, and he'll pay a great deal. But the deal was only good if we all sold. I was the only hold out, so—" I raised my hands. "He tried to persuade me with a knife to my throat."

Ian gazed, bemused, at the floor. The broken jar sat in a puddle, the broom by its side, along with two wooden knitting needles and a very feisty kitten, now grooming itself. "You fought off a trained killer wielding a knife with — knitting needles and a broom?"

"And my cat."

He shook his head. "I'll take a proper statement later, but for now, rest." He turned to go and then said, "Lucy, you are a remarkable woman."

As he was leaving, he said, "Oh, and I'm afraid we broke your door."

"I'm going to have to put that locksmith on speed dial."

NINETEEN

RAFE HELPED ME to my feet. "He's right, you know. You are a remarkable woman." I was about to answer when there was a rattle and fumbling and once more, the trap door began to open. My grandmother appeared, in black trousers and black T-shirt. Her hair was a mess and she looked as though she'd just woken up. She climbed up into the shop, then blinked and looked around. "Is it morning?"

I didn't know what to say. Rafe said, "It's six o'clock in the evening. Which is really your very early morning."

She shook her head. "This is like the worst jet lag I've ever had. I never know whether it's night or day."

"You'll get used to it," he said gently. "Perhaps you should go back to bed for a couple more hours."

"No." I said. "I'm really glad you're here, Gran. I think I found the grimoire."

Her face lit up. "That's wonderful, dear. I knew you would." Then she looked around at the broken glass, the broom on its side "Oh, dear. What a mess. What happened?"

"I'll explain. Go on upstairs and I'll be right there." Rafe led her into the shop, held the door open for her and she headed upstairs. I said, "I need to call the locksmith. Do you think they give a volume discount?"

"Relax, I know someone who works at night. He'll have it fixed by morning."

"Of course you do." I swept up the broken glass, put the broom back in its corner and returned the knitting needles to the basket. All in all, my vampire protection kit had worked better than I could have imagined.

I walked to the front part of the shop. "Maybe I can put something against the door handle until your locksmith gets here."

Before he could answer, the door flew open and Violet Weeks rushed in. She wore her long, black hair loose this time and the red and pink and purple stripe was like a birthday ribbon tracing her face. She wore loose black trousers, a blue silk shirt and a flowing garment that was a cross between a cloak and a coat. Instead of the ruby, she wore a large necklace of lapis lazuli and amethyst set in silver.

"Are you all right?" she asked, rushing to my side. "I heard there was a break in. My second sight told me you were in trouble."

I was not falling for the caring cousin act. I narrowed my eyes at her. "And my one and only sight tells me that you're a lying witch."

She opened her eyes and mouth wide.

"And you need to work on your fake outrage." I

stabbed my finger toward her chest. I was so mad sparks flew from my fingertips and danced on the lapis. "You stole my order book, and to do that you had to practically walk over my unconscious body."

She opened her mouth and I stabbed again until it looked like her necklace was putting on a fireworks display. "Do not even try to lie to me. I have a scrying mirror." I let her think I'd seen my order book in her home when really I was making an educated guess. "Who else but you could benefit from that grimoire? It's you who's been after it."

"All right, fine," she said, and put her palm in front of my finger before I could zap her again. "Stop that, it stings." She dug into her capacious bag and withdrew my order book. "I was bringing it back, if you must know. It's no good to me."

She kept glancing at Rafe, who was watching our fight with interest. "And who might you be?"

"This is my friend, Rafe Crosyer."

"Hmm," She glanced between us. "*Cosier*, I think you mean."

"Are you seriously going to make stupid puns when I was nearly killed and you didn't even try to save me? A killer knocked me out and you used the opportunity to steal the order book, thinking it was the grimoire."

"I checked to make sure you were breathing," she said haughtily. "And the man who'd attacked you was already running away so I knew you were safe."

"He could have come back," I grumbled.

"Well, he didn't. And I've brought your order book

back. I wasn't trying to *steal* the grimoire. It's as much mine as yours. My grandmother said so."

"On her deathbed, I suppose." I was still feeling irked with this woman and I didn't care to be polite.

"No. She's very much alive," said an older woman, stepping into the shop. She looked like Gran. Maybe she had a few more wrinkles, and her hair was more salt than pepper, but the remnants of the young woman I'd seen in Gran's family photos were there. "My granddaughter is correct. She has as much right to that grimoire as you do."

I had no idea what to do, so I said, "Why don't we go upstairs and sort this out." Then I remembered the broken door, and that I hadn't made it to the bank with the day's cash take. "As soon as we find a locksmith."

"Oh, for goddess's sake," the older witch snapped. She pointed her finger at the broken door and mumbled something, then she clapped her two hands together and held them. The door sparked and when the dazzle cleared, the door was shut and locked.

"Thank you," I said, though I still didn't think we were even for the leaving me to die thing.

Once more Rafe opened the door up to the flat and I led the way, followed by Violet Weeks and her grandmother. I had no idea what they would say when they discovered Gran appeared to be alive but I figured they were witches; they could just get used to it. At least, with Gran present, they couldn't pretend to things she knew to be false.

I didn't bother warning Gran about our visitors any

more than I bothered warning them about her. I merely got to the top of the stairs and led the way into the sitting room. I was pleased to see that in our absence Gran had made use of the cosmetics still in her bathroom, combed her hair, and slipped on one of the hand-knit sweaters that still hung in her closet.

Her eyes widened when she caught sight of our guests. She didn't look pleased. "Lavinia! What are you doing here?"

Violet Weeks's grandmother looked as startled as mine. "I might ask you the same question. You're supposed to be dead."

"You don't need to sound so happy about it. And I *am* dead."

Lavinia walked closer to my grandmother and sniffed the air. "A vampire. Didn't our mother teach you anything? What happened to your protection spells?"

My grandmother rose and put her hands on her hips. "And what happened to your manners? You know you're not welcome here."

Her sister crossed her arms and the two old witches faced each other. Lavinia said, "We find ourselves in an interesting dilemma. The grimoire was our mother's and belongs equally to our granddaughters."

Gran shook her head. "No, it doesn't. Mother handed it to me when you turned dark. Your own mother didn't trust you and I certainly don't."

There was some serious animosity in the room and Nyx circled around my ankles until I picked her up. I wasn't sure whether she was offering comfort or wanting it but I was happy to hold her in my arms. She didn't purr as she usually did when I picked her up. she held herself stiff, her ears pointing straight up and her eyes wide open. I felt at any moment she was ready to launch herself out of my arms and attack if necessary.

I really, really hoped it wouldn't be. I don't like conflict at the best of times, and Lavinia and Violet were the only living relatives I seemed to have in the UK. If there was a way to work out these old conflicts, I'd be happy to do so.

Gran said, "If you thought your granddaughter was entitled to the grimoire, why were you so intent on stealing it?"

Lavinia coloured slightly. "Perhaps that was beneath me. But Violet is the next generation of our family and she needs it for her education. I never saw any sign that your granddaughter had the gift."

Gran sniffed and looked unconvinced. We seemed to have reached a standoff. "I knew you were after it before I died, so I hid the book. After I was turned, I couldn't remember where I put it."

Lavinia looked genuinely concerned. She stepped forward, "Agnes, this can't be true. If that book fell into the wrong hands, if dark forces were unleashed, well, that's one of the reasons I wanted to safeguard it."

Gran glanced at me, looking triumphant. "Lucy found it. Without my help."

She looked so relieved. And so did Lavinia. The cat jumped out of my arms and headed toward my bedroom, as though she were giving me permission to reveal the book to these rival witches. I followed and, tossing the extra bedding aside, retrieved the grimoire from my suitcase. I returned with the book and Gran said, "Oh, thank goodness you found it. Where was it?"

"You hid it well. It was next door with the Miss Watts."

She nodded, enthusiastic. "Yes. Now I remember. They never look in those crowded old bookshelves, so I just slipped the book up on top. I knew that no one would ever look for it there."

Lavinia nearly snatched the book out of my hands. She ran her fingers reverently over the old leather cover. "I remember how we used to giggle and fight as we tried to outdo each other with the spells," she said, her voice softening.

Gran stepped closer to her. "You usually caught on faster, which always annoyed me."

"You were younger. But once you mastered the spell, yours was usually the more powerful."

She turned the book over in her hands. "Violet's a good witch. I want her to learn from our ancestors. Read our history, and practice our ancient art."

Gran said, "And I want that for Lucy."

Lavinia looked from me to Gran. "How much practice has Lucy had? She's been living away from our people. Has she had a mentor? Is her mother a practicing witch?"

I had a sneaking feeling she already knew the answers to these questions and that only made her granddaughter seem like the proper recipient of the book. I waited. I knew something they didn't.

Inevitably, Lavinia tried to open the cover of the book. It resisted her efforts as easily as it had resisted mine. She frowned and sniffed. "This book is spellbound."

She turned to her sister and once again the antagonism crackled between them. "I demand that you open this book by removing the spell."

Gran shook her head. "When I was turned into a vampire, I lost a great deal of my memories and most of my power. I couldn't even remember where I hid the book, how on earth can I remember the spell I put upon it?"

Lavinia began smile. "That's how our mother decided between us, in the end. She put a spell on this very book and whoever could break that spell was destined to carry it with her for life."

"Exactly," Gran said.

Lavinia touched the book's cover again. "It seems fitting then that our two granddaughters should be offered the same challenge. If one of these young witches can break the spell, then the book is meant for her."

But she wasn't throwing this idea out as a fair challenge between equals. Putting me up against Violet was like throwing a puny kid into the boxing ring with a heavyweight prize fighter.

I said, "But I didn't even know I was a witch until a few days ago. I have no training, I've never broken a spell in my life, I've never even set one. This is completely unfair."

I turned to Gran, who had settled herself on the couch and wore an inscrutable expression. I noticed then that the photo album was open on the table. It had been closed when I left this morning. Clearly, she had been looking at photographs of her past and, perhaps, the pictures of her and her sister as youngsters had softened her towards her old enemy.

I wasn't at all sure about these two, however. Violet had all but stepped over my corpse so anxious was she to get hold of that grimoire. Was this the kind of witch who should control the power held between those old leather covers?

Violet sent me a smug and superior glance that made me long to hit her. Lavinia said, "Nonsense. A witch's power is inherent. You can learn a great deal from this book, but a witch with inborn power and a pure heart can certainly break another witch's spell."

I did not believe her. I was positive that both she and her smug granddaughter considered this contest already won. I could picture them sitting cozily around their cauldron, no doubt making potions that would put warts on my face. I felt as sulky as Hester, especially when Gran didn't jump to my defence.

I wondered if, now that she was a vampire, she had forgotten her connection to my world, the world of humans and of witches.

I turned to Rafe. He was a sensible, intelligent vampire. Surely he could see what was going on here. "Rafe. Tell them this isn't fair. I need more time to prepare."

He shrugged his elegant shoulders. "I never get involved in witch matters."

I felt almost desperate. I wanted that grimoire. I wanted to learn how to be a powerful witch, to revere the earth, heal people, help the lovelorn find their mates and whatever else it was witches did. I wanted to help protect the innocent from evil. I said, "There must be some sort of witch government, who could oversee this."

In one voice my grandmother and my great-aunt cried, "No." Then they glanced at each other and Gran said, "There are, of course, governing bodies, but this is a family matter. This grimoire is an old and powerful book, and we do not want run-of-the-mill witches to know about it. Lucy, I'm sorry you haven't had more training, but remember everything I told you."

She looked at me then with her wise, old eyes and I realized that she still cared very much about me and my world. I felt a lightening around my heart as I realized that she believed in me. She thought, even without the years of training that Violet had no doubt undergone, that I had a shot at this.

Nyx was regarding me with equally clear, wise eyes. "All right," I said, resigned. "Tell me how this works?"

Lavinia said, "It's very simple. Each of you will try to break the spell. Whoever succeeds gets the book."

"And if neither of us can do it?"

The old witches glanced at each other. Lavinia said,

"Then, I suppose, your grandmother and I will each take a turn and if neither of us can break the spell, the book will have to be destroyed."

"No!" Both Violet and I cried out.

Lavinia drilled us each with her gaze. "Then, one of you had better open this book."

We tossed a coin to decide who went first. It seemed very pedestrian, but I suppose it was as fair as any other method. Rafe was chosen as the coin tosser. Violet called heads and I took tails. He withdrew a twenty-pence piece from his pocket, showed it to all of us, and then flicked it up into the air. I don't know whether Violet or her grandmother cast a spell on the coin as it was flying up into the air, but it came down heads, which was what Violet had chosen.

Lavinia had all of us witches sit in a circle, the book in the center. Gran fetched candles and lit them. It felt both cozy, mysterious and mystical sitting in that circle with the candlelight flickering off that old magic book. I felt a shiver ran over my body and Nyx came and curled herself into my lap.

I felt the power of us four witches sitting in the circle. Rafe stood outside its light, since he was neither witch nor mortal.

"Should we join hands?" Lavinia asked, looking at Gran.

My grandmother seemed to debate then she said, "No. Let each witch's magic remain with her."

Lavinia nodded and then said to Violet, "Now, take your time. Focus. Blessed be."

If Violet was nervous she certainly didn't show it. There was a serenity, and a confidence to her as she closed her eyes and reached her two hands out towards the book. She said,

Gift of the protector I return to thee,
Let this book opened be.

I think we all held our breath, and then Violet leaned forward onto her hands and knees, and reached for the book. She placed her hand on it and lifted the cover. The entire book lifted, the pages as stuck together as though it were a sculpture of a book and not the real thing.

"Wait," Violet said. "I didn't concentrate properly. Let me try again."

"It's Lucy's turn, now," Gran said.

"But she'll copy me, and it's not fair. She doesn't even know how to break a spell."

I felt Nyx's warm body against mine. She was purring, so softly only I could hear her, more vibration than noise. Gran's gaze was steady on me. Nobody had to tell me that it would be foolish to copy Violet's attempt, which hadn't even worked.

I closed my eyes and went down into myself. I saw myself in the knitting shop with Gran, the balls of wool dancing around under my spell. I pictured myself fighting off a killer earlier today, and that sense of power I'd felt. I would use my power for good, I promised. I felt open and ready for whatever lay ahead. I was part of the earth and nature, not a creator of power, but its conduit. I said,

Magic grimoire, if I am meant to be the next in line,
Then open your heart as I open mine.

I opened my eyes then, feeling a little foolish at my extemporaneous and very simple rhyme. I hadn't intended them, the words had simply come out of me. I pictured the book opening and revealing its pages to me and as I leaned forward, golden light began to spill from within as the book opened of its own accord, to a page covered with symbols and faded words.

"She did it," Lavinia said softly, sounding amazed. "Lucy, it's your turn to carry the grimoire. Use it wisely, my dear, and let us help you as we can."

Then she rose and said, "Come along, Violet. It's time for us to go."

Violet didn't even argue. She nodded and rose to her feet. "Good luck, Lucy. Blessed be."

"Wait," I said. "You're my family. I think it's time we got to know each other. I've got an attic full of photographs from when you, Aunt Lavinia, and Gran, were young." I put my hands on my hips. "I've also got the phone number of a local pizza place. The grocer's still open and they sell wine. Please, stay, let me get to know you."

Lavinia looked to Gran. "Agnes?"

I watched the two sisters staring warily at each other. Finally my grandmother said, "Two generations have passed. Maybe it's time to heal old wounds."

Lavinia turned to me with a wry smile on her face. "I think, young lady, you've already shown yourself to be a very promising witch."

Violet rolled her eyes. "Please use your powers to order some pizza. I'm starving. And, since you get the grimoire, you're buying."

I laughed, and lifted Nyx from my lap so I could go and get my mobile. "I'm on it."

I'd arrived in Oxford lost and broken-hearted, hoping Gran could give me a shoulder to cry on and a quiet place to heal. In the short time I'd been here, I'd helped solve two murders, though officially only one, made friends with both living and undead, discovered I was a witch, and even found a second family.

I couldn't imagine another week to rival this one.

Nyx made a noise as though she was coughing up a fur ball and silver and gold sparks sprayed out of her mouth.

Oh, yeah. And, I got adopted by the most amazing, magical cat ever.

ALSO BY NANCY WARREN

The best way to keep up with new releases, plus enjoy bonus content and prizes is to join Nancy's newsletter at www.nancywarren.net.

TAKE A CHANCE SERIES

Meet the chance family, a cobbled together family of eleven kids who are all grown up and finding their ways in life and love.

Chance Encounter, Prequel
Kiss a Girl in the Rain, Book 1
Iris in Bloom, Book 2
Blueprint for a Kiss, Book 3
Every Rose, Book 4
Love to Go, Book 5
The Daisy Game, Book 6

THE ALMOST WIVES CLUB

An enchanted wedding dress is a matchmaker in this series of romantic comedies where five runaway brides find out who the best men really are!

The Almost Wives Club: Kate, Book 1
Second Hand Bride, Book 2

Bridesmaid for Hire, Book 3
The Wedding Flight, Book 4
If the Dress Fits, Book 5

TONI DIAMOND MYSTERIES

Toni is a successful saleswoman for Lady Bianca Cosmetics in this series of humorous cozy mysteries. Along with having an eye for beauty and a head for business, Toni's got a nose for trouble and she's never shy about following her instincts, even when they lead to murder.

Frosted Shadow, Book One
Ultimate Concealer, Book Two
Midnight Shimmer, Book Three

A Diamond Choker For Christmas,
A Toni Diamond Mysteries Novella

For a complete list of books, check out Nancy's website at www.nancywarren.net.

ABOUT THE AUTHOR

Nancy Warren is the USA Today Bestselling author of more than 70 novels. She's originally from Vancouver, Canada, though she tends to wander and has lived in England, Italy and California at various times. Favorite moments include being the answer to a crossword puzzle clue in Canada's National Post newspaper, being featured on the front page of the New York Times when her book Speed Dating launched Harlequin's NASCAR series, and being nominated three times for Romance Writers of America's RITA award. She's an avid hiker, loves chocolate and most of all, loves to hear from readers! The best way to stay in touch is to sign up for Nancy's newsletter at www.nancywarren.net.

Learn more about Nancy and her books:

Twitter: @nancywarren1
Facebook: www.facebook.com/Nancy-Warren
Website: www.nancywarren.net
Email: nancyYwarren@gmail.com

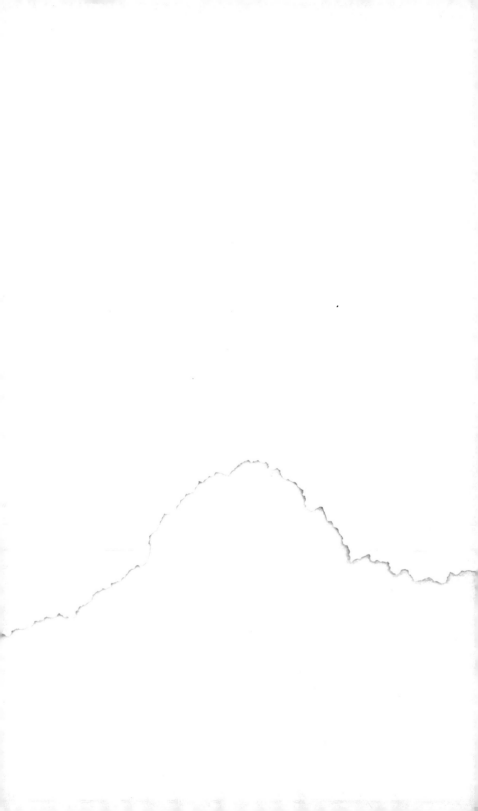

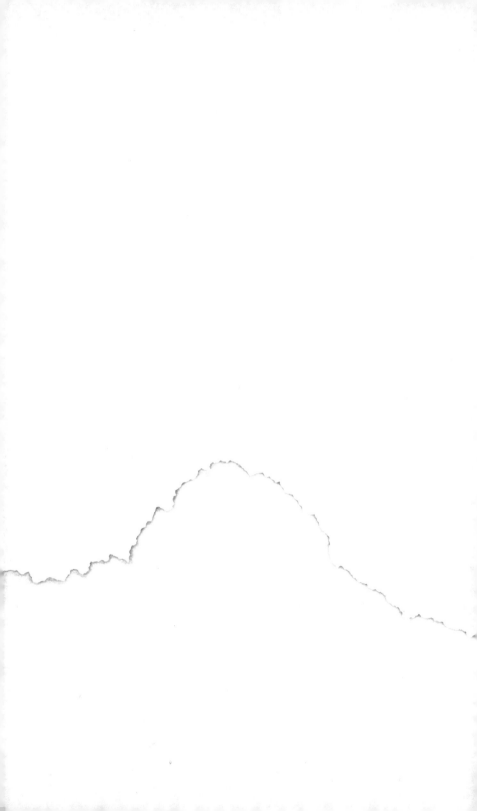

Made in the USA
Lexington, KY
10 December 2018